Books by Jo Dereske

Glom Gloom
The Lone Sentinel

A JEAN KARL BOOK

ATHENEUM 1989
NEW YORK

TO K.L.W.

ATHENEUM
Macmillan Publishing Company
866 Third Avenue, New York, NY 10022
Collier Macmillan Canada, Inc.

First Edition
Printed in the United States of America
Designed by Michael Ian Kaye
10 9 8 7 6 5 4 3 2 1

Library of Congress Cataloging-in-Publication Data
Dereske, Jo.
The lone sentinel.
"A Jean Karl book."
Summary: At his father's untimely death,
a teenager assumes control of a light tower
at a bleak and lonely outpost of the universe
—a job he feels capable of handling until
the arrival of two teenaged girls and a
group of aliens.
[1. Science fiction] I. Title.
PZ7.D4418Lo 1989 [Fic] 88–36254
ISBN 0–689–31552–X

CONTENTS

1
THE STORM

"Do you think the storm's getting worse, Dad?" Erik asked, setting down his fork and raising his voice above the sounds of the wind buffeting the little metal house.

Erik's father stood in front of the window, his hands clasped behind his back, his eyes raised toward the Lone Sentinel's beam high atop the steel tower.

"It's one of the worst I've seen in all the years I've been a careman," he said. "Azure's winters aren't known for their hospitality. I remember one ice storm fourteen years ago, when you were a baby; it wrapped the house in an ice cocoon. When we opened the door, we had to break through a wall of ice to get out."

Through the window, the steady sweep of light from the sentinel's beam crossed the dark afternoon sky, illuminating the thick, blowing snow and sleet.

Erik's father hadn't touched his dinner. The storm had begun unexpectedly that morning, descending so heavily that the short day existed as a gloomy twilight,

■ 1 ■

full of howling wind and icy snowflakes that blew from every direction.

After they'd completed their daily check of the Lone Sentinel compound and the mechanisms of the sentinel itself, Erik and his father had spent the day inside reading, watching videos, playing two games of chess, but always with an ear or an eye to the storm.

"Should we do another check?" Erik asked, pushing away his half-finished dinner.

His father turned from the window, rubbing the back of his neck and smiling.

"I think you'd actually like to go out in this, wouldn't you? We can do a short check before we go to bed, just to be sure the wind and ice haven't been a strain on the mechanisms."

The wind shrieked, and the house shuddered as if it were tearing loose. A crash sounded outside the near room, where they kept their winter clothes and tools. At Erik's feet, Thursday growled warily and sat up.

Erik reached under the table and rubbed the thick fur behind Thursday's ears. She quieted and leaned her head against his leg.

"That must have been the snow-shovel rack going over," his father said. "We can right it later when we go out."

He dropped into the Reclina-Chair and stretched his legs on the foot rest. His black hair bushed out around his face. It was time to give each other haircuts.

Erik left the table and sat in the Reclina-Chair opposite his father. The chair had once belonged to his mother; now it was Erik's.

The beam passed over and brightened the window. The icy snow hit against the double-paned glass like sand.

"Have you finished the Kipling series?" his father asked, his eyes toward the window.

"Almost. I have one story left in *Plain Tales from the Hills,* and I'll be ready to write my paper."

"Good," he said warmly, but Erik knew his father's attention was on the storm, not on Erik's studies. "I'm pleased you're keeping up with the schedule."

"I'm even ahead of it. When Chad comes this year, I might have enough work completed to be moved into the top level."

Erik had never been inside a school, but he'd seen videos of the noisy classrooms in New Province. He preferred his own solitary way of doing his lessons, but at the same time, he felt a nudge of satisfaction at being ahead of the New Province students who had all those teachers to help them.

Erik closed his eyes and leaned back. The wind rose and howled in a sorrowful cry. The day felt timeless, without morning or evening, only weather.

"There it is," Erik's father said in a tight voice that barely carried over the wailing storm.

Erik jerked upright in his chair, his heart thumping.

His father stood tensely in front of the window. The beam held stationary to the east, a slice of light in the clouds and swirling snow.

"It stopped," Erik whispered.

Over the years, there had been problems on the Lone Sentinel, but he couldn't recall the beam ever stopping.

"The high gear," his father said. "I suspected this might happen with the combined ice and wind."

They stood side by side at the window. Erik willed the beam to break free and continue its sweep of light across the blackened sky, but it didn't move.

"We could wait until tomorrow to repair it," Erik said. "No predator will bother the biosote during this storm."

Erik's father shook his head. "The beam is the careman's responsibility—every second." He turned to Erik. "I'll inform the Trust. You get the equipment ready."

As he carried their tools and winter garb in an armload from the near room, Erik heard his father on the radio.

"Beam holding at sixty-three-degree incline, ninety-six-degree rotation. Suspect the high gear."

The radio crackled, interrupting the transmission.

" . . . report when inspection is completed," the voice from Trust Control ordered.

"Affirmative. Lone Sentinel clear."

"Trust Control clear."

Silently, his father put on the thick, specially soled boots used to climb the sentinel's steel-runged ladder. Erik pulled on his own identical boots, his fingers fumbling with the catches. The winds dropped to a sudden stillness. Erik held his breath in the silence. Thursday whined, and the winds returned, slamming into the house, rattling the windows and walls.

"That was a good one," Erik's father said, glancing up at the ceiling.

Erik swallowed the dryness in his throat. He held out his father's bulky winter jacket, opening it so he could back his arms into the sleeves, but his father motioned it away.

"It'll just get in the way while I'm climbing." He smiled at Erik. "I'll have the high gear repaired before I even have a chance to get cold. I'll wear the mitts, though."

When Erik stepped out the door behind his father, the shrieking gusts blew his breath back into his throat. The snow had lessened, but the wind drove it against his face. He scrunched his eyes to slits and pulled the collar of his jacket over his mouth. Thursday walked close beside Erik with her head and tail low.

The familiar landmarks of the Lone Sentinel compound loomed in the evening dimness, driven to threatening proportions by the howling weather. Erik couldn't see a trace of the biosote fields that stretched up and across Green Grass Ridge. He was sure that the struckies and the borers wouldn't brave this weather for a taste of the biosote.

At the foot of the sentinel's ladder, Erik's father checked the tool belt around his waist and squinted up at the distant stationary beam. Icy snow already crusted his cap.

"If it can't be easily repaired, I'll come back down," he shouted close to Erik's ear.

Erik nodded, knowing his words would be lost in the thick fur of his collar and the angry winds.

His father squeezed Erik's shoulder through the heavy jacket and began the ascent.

Erik protected his eyes from the sharp flakes and watched his father feel his way up the ice-coated steel ladder, arm over arm and foot over foot, slowly scaling the Lone Sentinel's graceful structure. In the storm and early darkness, only the light of the eerily stopped beam let Erik see the small form working its way upward.

Again the winds fell silent. The snowflakes paused and drifted lazily to earth, leaving the night unnaturally quiet, with Erik's father a third of the way up the sentinel.

He should have expected it.

With a roar, the ice-blown wind came to life again. It caught Erik's father between rungs, feet reaching for the next crosspiece, while Erik stood below with his hands cupped around his eyes, watching.

His father danced with the wind for an impossibly long instant, appearing for a moment as if he might defy both gravity and the howling air. His legs kicked out as if his knees were jointed backward. His arms clutched the sides of the ladder. One let go and waved to the wind's tune while the other held tight. Then it, too, let go.

"Dad!" Erik shouted, but his cry blew back at him, hardly more than a whisper.

His father was swept out on the wind. It held him, toying, then discarded him, flinging him back against the metal rungs and tumbling him to the snow-covered ground.

Erik should have stopped his father from climbing the sentinel. He should have warned him that the ladder was too icy to climb, the wind too strong. He dropped to his knees in the snow beside his father. He was helpless, useless to change what had happened. His father was dead.

He took off his jacket and covered his father, first brushing the snow from his face and straightening his arms, talking to him. He hardly knew what he said; his mind roared like the storm around him.

"Why didn't you hold on tighter? The winds . . . Couldn't you see how dangerous . . . " Erik sat beside his father, resting his hand on the jacket. Thursday circled them, growling uncertainly, her snowy hackles raised.

"The beam is the careman's responsibility—every second," his father had said.

Finally, in his sweater, without a jacket or mitts, Erik climbed the sentinel himself. He groped his way up the rungs his father had climbed so easily minutes earlier, fighting the ice and gusts of wind until he reached the high gear. With his hands growing numb, he repaired the jammed mechanism while the snow stung his cheeks like ice shards. He barely noticed. All of him, his body and his mind, felt equally numb.

On the way down, he saw Thursday lying beside the dark shape on the ground, surely too small to be his father.

"The high gear is repaired, and the Lone Sentinel's beam is on its prescribed track," Erik said wearily into the radio.

"Anything further to report?"

"Negative. Lone Sentinel clear."

"Trust Control clear."

Erik slumped in the chair in front of the radio. His hands ached from the cold, mottled with red. He rubbed them together and put them under his arms.

Then he made himself think it.

His father was dead. He was gone.

His father.

His father was dead and he, Erik, hadn't informed Trust Control.

Outside, the storm was blowing itself out. The wind had loosened its hold as if it had completed its mission and was rushing off to another, more challenging assignment.

Erik stood and peered into the mirror above the radio. His black hair was tangled and damp, still dripping melted snow down his forehead. His blue eyes were a stranger's, wide and haunted. White spots showed on his cheeks. All of his skin seemed gray.

His father was dead, and he was alone hundreds of miles from New Province. On top of that, he had lied to Trust Control.

His father wouldn't have lied, not to Trust Control, and not to Erik.

Would the Trust suspect? Erik's voice had already changed to its deeper register, and he knew he sounded enough like his father to pass for him over the radio.

If the Trust found out his father was dead, they'd arrange for his replacement. They'd take Erik off the Lone Sentinel and send him to live with strangers in New Province. He'd probably never see the Lone Sentinel again. But the Lone Sentinel was his home. He knew nothing else. He couldn't imagine any other life.

Yet none of that would matter to Trust Control. Too much could go wrong, they'd say. Erik was only fourteen, too young. The aloneness might come on him. There could be an accident, they'd reason, or an emergency he didn't have the experience to handle. They'd be sorry, but the rules would have to be followed.

In the silent and empty house, Erik knelt on the floor beside Thursday and pulled her head into his lap. She licked Erik's hand as he put his face down into her heavy coat.

The next night, after he'd said the funeral ceremony from the Trust Operations Manual, Erik watched the red flames of his father's funeral pyre reach toward the sky as the Lone Sentinel's beam crossed above him.

The only sounds in the calm darkness were the crackling of the flames and the steady whirring of the sentinel's mechanisms. The frigid northern night was gently starlit. Erik peered up at the millions of stars in the moonless sky, wondering briefly if the planet Earth still existed among the points of light.

He knew the surrounding stark scenery too well to feel uneasy, but the surge of lonely sorrow was new to him. He moved closer to the warmth of the pyre.

"Farewell, Dad," Erik said solemnly.

2
ROUTINES

"Erik."

"I'm here," Erik answered, sitting up expectantly in bed.

The beam was on the opposite end of its arc, and his bedroom was dark. Thursday lay stretched across his feet, sound asleep.

"I'm here," he said again, knowing as he said it that there couldn't be anyone calling him. He peered around his small bedroom, into the shadowed corners by his bookcases.

After two months of being alone, was this the aloneness touching him? He strained to hear the voice, telling himself it was impossible, but still listening, his teeth clenched and his hands balling up the blankets.

The shadows around his bureau shifted and changed shape as the beam's light passed. Erik prodded Thursday with his foot until she heaved a deep sigh and sleepily nuzzled his hand.

For the rest of the long night he lay awake, rigid in his bed, watching the arrow of the Lone Sentinel's beam travel through the darkness and listening to the low wind and the humming undercurrent of the sentinel's mechanisms. There were no other sounds, no voices, nothing unusual.

Erik's life had fallen into a routine that formed his days. He rarely varied his schedule, satisfied to know what he would be doing each hour of each day. Sometimes now, when he thought of his father he smiled.

Every day after eating breakfast and feeding Thursday, he put on his jacket, stuffed his mitts into his pockets, and went to the shed that squatted beneath the Lone Sentinel. Just as he and his father had done, he checked the complicated mechanisms that ran the beam, saying each item aloud and inspecting it before he slashed it on the checklist. Thursday stayed within arm's reach, sometimes dozing to the drone of Erik's voice.

Once a week, he climbed the ladder all the way to the top of the two-hundred-foot sentinel, always keeping one foot on a rung until his other foot was firmly on the next rung, never taking his hands from the sides, slowly making his way up the dizzying height. So he wouldn't be afraid, so he would be sure of his step. And not fall.

Every morning he walked the perimeters of the Lone Sentinel compound, examining the earth for signs of borers, the big rodents that burrowed through the ground and could weaken the earth around the sentinel. When the borers were especially active, Erik carried a small gun his father had taught him to use.

Then he hiked up to the fields on Green Grass Ridge where the biosote grew. The rock-hard biosote subtly changed hue with the seasons: from icy pink in spring to dusky rose in winter, darkening each year until by the end of its ten-year growth cycle the fields would glow a deep red.

Every ten years the Helgatites returned to the six sentinels on Azure to gather the mature biosote and transport it back to their own planet. The summer he was eight, Erik had watched through the windows as his father helped the thin silvery figures in the biosote fields. The Helgatites couldn't live in Azure's atmosphere without their protective suits, but even the suits didn't protect them from extreme exhaustion. The Helgatites stayed on Azure only long enough to gather the biosote.

Biosote was of no use to the colonists, but the Helgatites couldn't live without it. They'd begun gathering biosote centuries ago, first for pleasure, but now their lives depended on it.

"The first time the Helgatites saw you," Erik's father had told him, "they wanted to know all about you, to assure themselves that you were healthy."

"Could they have fixed me if I hadn't been?"

"Some say they could. Some say the Helgatites have skills we cannot even imagine."

"Then why do they need us, or the sentinels?" Erik had asked.

"Because they're too fragile to stay on Azure and protect the biosote until it matures. Before the earthlings came to Azure, the biosote grew wild. Much of it was destroyed by predators."

Every child learned the story of how the earthlings had been too eager to colonize and claim Azure. When inadequate supplies and the first harsh winter caught the colonists unprepared and light-years from their home planet, the Helgatites had risked their lives to help them.

When the danger had passed, the grateful colonists worked together with the Helgatites to develop the Trust Control system with its six sentinels and six cultivated biosote fields. Overhead, a Helgatite satellite station orbited Azure to protect the colonists from possible invaders. By the time of the last war, when all contact with Earth was lost, the relationship between the colonists of New Province and the Helgatites was firmly established.

There were intelligent beings on many scattered planets, Erik knew. But the humans on Azure had dealings only with the Helgatites. That was part of the original agreement between New Province and the Helgatites. Azure was a closed planet, an island, its inhabitants living as close as possible to extinct Earth ways.

The voice he'd heard in the night seemed like a silly dream the next morning. Nothing had changed. Snow and ice still covered the upper reaches of the biosote fields. The frozen grasses crunched under his feet. He kicked a rock as he walked through the biosote making sure that no predators had evaded the beam and entered the fields. The rock clattered against the solid biosote.

Thursday barked at the rolling rock, then tipped her head expectantly at Erik, her tail wagging.

"We'll throw the ball later, Thursday," he said. "We have work to do now."

The beam swung past, just touching the top of Green Grass Ridge. The beam discouraged the natural predators of the biosote: the borers, and the large flying struckies, who found the newest growth a delicacy. The struckies were bigger than Erik, but they were too graceless to be taken seriously. Only the appetites of the borers and struckies were dangerous; they were as shy of the caremen as they were of the beam.

In its normal state, the beam carried a slight charge that frightened the predators, but there were other more powerful and dangerous levels, levels that Erik knew how to program but only the Trust and the Helgatites fully understood.

Thursday dug excitedly at the frozen ground.

"Good, Thursday," Erik praised. He stamped along the raised earth of a borer tunnel, collapsing it. That was usually enough to send the timid borers racing back through their burrow, abandoning it.

After Erik finished the check of the Lone Sentinel compound he inspected the generator that ran his house, and the temperature and humidity of the supply room where his year's supplies were stored.

Finally, he waited nervously by the radio for the daily Trust Broadcast. Was this the day he'd be found out? So far, Trust Control hadn't questioned whether he was his father. The ban against personal conversation saved Erik from having to speak more than the briefest sentences.

"Trust Broadcast," came the voice over the radio. "Please acknowledge."

Each sentinel responded in turn.

"Willow Sentinel acknowledges."

"Green Sentinel acknowledges."

"Triumph Sentinel acknowledges."

"Bay Sentinel acknowledges."

"Copper Sentinel acknowledges."

Erik clicked the blue response button, cleared his throat, and said in his deepest voice, "Lone Sentinel acknowledges."

After the general announcements, Trust Control transmitted to each sentinel individually—and privately. Erik was last and had to wait longest.

"Lone Sentinel," came the call from Trust Control.

"Lone Sentinel here," Erik said. Beside him, Thursday sat up and tipped her ears forward.

"Report."

"Winds at five to seven knots. Temperature: five degrees Fahrenheit. Rotation at sixty-three degrees. No oscillation."

"Accepted, Lone Sentinel. A party of three hunters, led by Wayne Burdick, will be traveling through your area next week. Notify Trust Control if they fail to report in ten days. Any additional reports?"

"Negative," Erik said. "Information acknowledged."

He kept his voice calm, but panic raced through him. Strangers coming to the Lone Sentinel. Already.

This time of the year was usually a dry, frozen pause between the snows and the melt, a time when a few hunting parties from New Province made the trip to hunt beyond the Lone Sentinel for the thick-pelted creatures that the earthlings called bears. Erik had always stayed out of the way, letting his father deal with the passing hunters and the few visitors who stopped at the Lone Sentinel.

If only his father were there to meet the hunters, to . . . Erik shook his head. He couldn't think those thoughts. His father was gone. Thinking like that invited the aloneness.

Even though his mind wasn't on it, Erik kept to his daily routine and took one plastic-wrapped, year-old New Province newspaper from the stack just inside the supply room. The newspapers were delivered every autumn when Chad the supplier delivered the rest of the year's supplies.

The words in the newspaper were gone from his mind as soon as he read them. He set it aside and tried to study his geometry, but that was worse; the theorems and proofs were only gibberish. Even watching *A Midsummer Night's Dream* on video for his literature studies felt meaningless.

Strangers were coming to the Lone Sentinel.

He knew he had kept to the schedule. The Lone Sentinel compound was firmly in order; the biosote was growing according to schedule. He had very carefully followed every rule and suggestion in the Trust Operations Manual, hoping that by doing everything else right, the one rule he'd broken wouldn't be discovered.

But now a hunting party was on its way to the Lone Sentinel. Erik couldn't remember Wayne Burdick, the party's leader, but he might have visited the Lone Sentinel before. He was sure to know the Trust rule that a sentinel be manned by more than one person. What would Wayne Burdick do when he discovered Erik was alone?

Erik looked around his house. The circular rhythm of the Lone Sentinel's beam above him was like a heartbeat. Here was his home, here and nowhere else.

Thursday pawed at Erik, her red ball in her mouth. He tugged at the ball, but she held tight, playfully growling as she pulled against him.

"You must be able to tell time, Thursday," Erik said. It was just past three o'clock, the time he usually took Thursday outside for exercise.

The slanting rays of the sun deepened the shadows of the sentinel into grids across the compound. Thursday chased the ball tirelessly, dropping it at Erik's feet and eagerly waiting for him to toss it again.

"This is the last time," Erik warned sternly, and threw the ball as hard as he could.

Thursday barked and lunged after it as it rolled along the frozen ground toward the edge of the compound.

But suddenly she stopped and peered tensely toward Green Grass Ridge, the ball forgotten. The fur on her back bristled as she stood on stiff legs, rumbling growls coming from her throat.

Erik squinted and made out the dark shapes of two wolves traversing above the biosote on Green Grass Ridge. The animals were called wolves because they closely resembled Earth wolves, except that these wolves were browner, with longer ears and broader bodies.

Thursday whined, watching the wolves. She wagged her tail once, turned skittishly in a circle, and growled again.

"Thursday," Erik called softly, not moving.

Thursday was half wolf. Four years earlier, Thursday's mother had disappeared for a week. When she returned, it was soon apparent she would have puppies. There had been four, and although they tried every means they knew, Erik and his father had managed to save only one. At the time, Erik had been reading his favorite book, *Robinson Crusoe,* and because the puppies were born on a Thursday, he'd named the last puppy Thursday.

Erik watched Thursday closely as the two wolves disappeared into the shadows on the other side of the biosote fields. If Thursday ran after them, if she left him, he'd be truly alone.

Thursday turned and looked at Erik, whined once more toward Green Grass Ridge, and picked up her ball.

"Good girl, good girl," he said when she dropped the ball in front of him.

Then he threw the ball for her until it was too dark to see.

3
THE HUNTERS

Erik stood at the edge of the compound, waiting. He brushed his hair off his forehead. The unnatural sounds of a groaning engine and shifting gears had been reaching him on the breezes for half an hour.

He'd never seen the road between New Province and the Lone Sentinel, but he knew it must be muddy after the sudden warming of the past few days. Snow still lay in the shadows, but where the sun could reach, a few spears of green showed through the brown.

His father had been dead for three months; it was three months since Erik had looked another person in the face. What would Wayne Burdick and his fellow hunters be like?

Erik sat on a boulder and scuffed his feet in the soft ground. His duty was to the Lone Sentinel, not to the approaching strangers; they could only disrupt his careful routine. They could only be danger. Yet it was the job, too, of caremen to be hospitable. He stood up and practiced saying "Hello" and "Welcome to the Lone Sentinel," while the motor sounds growled toward him.

As the afternoon breezes gathered force, a flat-topped gray vehicle lurched from between the low hills to the south, a heavily loaded, back-road vehicle. A tarp was lashed over supplies on the roof. Erik didn't have to see the guns to know that here were the hunters.

The muddy vehicle braked in the shadow of the sentinel, its motor dying in a harsh groan. Behind Erik, from inside the metal house, Thursday barked frantically.

The driver's door opened. In the spring air that felt so balmy to Erik that he wore only a shirt over his thermal undershirt, the driver had on a lined jacket and a hat with fur muffs that covered his ears. When he swung out of his vehicle, Erik saw his fur-lined boots.

"Hello!" the hunter called, heartily waving his arm.

"Hello," Erik said around the thickness in his throat, just the way he'd practiced it.

The hunter smiled, walking toward Erik with one hand out while he took off his hat with the other. He was tall, taller than Erik's father; his face was tanned and lined, emphasized by a sandy mustache and bright blue eyes.

"You're a fine sight, Careman," the hunter said. "The last leg of our trip was a muddy mess."

Erik shook the hunter's hand, feeling his strong grip. He tried to speak but couldn't. A stiff smile stretched his face, and his vision unexplainably fogged.

"We've driven hard today, trying to make up for lost time. May we spend tonight with you?" the hunter asked, waving toward the vehicle. "There are three of us."

Erik cleared his throat. "I'd be honored if . . . Please." His voice sounded too loud. "Your gear, can I help?"

"We'd be grateful for a hand. The longer you travel, the heavier your gear seems to grow. My name's Burdick."

The other two hunters, one Burdick's height but heavier, the other a white-haired and bearded man who walked with a slight stoop, climbed from the vehicle and came forward, stretching their arms and backs.

"This is Alan," Burdick said, nodding to the heavy man, "and this is his father, Joseph."

"Welcome to the Lone Sentinel," Erik said, stuttering a little.

"It's good to see you, young man," the white-haired Joseph said. "I was beginning to wonder if Burdick here really *did* know his way."

Erik stepped back from the three men and their big voices, their open questioning faces. They looked at him expectantly. Erik looked at the ground. What were they waiting for? What had he forgotten?

"And your name, Careman?" Burdick asked politely.

That was all. He hadn't told them his name.

"I am Erik. Welcome to the Lone Sentinel," he repeated.

"Is your father here?" Burdick asked.

Erik shook his head. His hopes sank. Burdick did know his father, then. The three men were still too close; he took another step back.

"He went over the Green Grass Ridge to check old borer traps. He'll be gone overnight." Erik's voice felt mechanical, unused—and untruthful.

"We'll be sorry to miss him," Alan said.

Burdick nodded. "I've visited with him when I've brought other hunting parties up this way. Last time I was here, you were about this high," he said, holding his hand at waist level. "I'll bet you're as tall as he is now." Burdick laughed. "Your father's a good chess player. I was looking forward to a game."

"I've rarely beat him," Erik said.

"If you've *ever* beat him, you must be a fine player. Would you consider a game tonight?"

"I'd be honored," Erik told him.

Before they carried the hunters' gear inside, Erik locked Thursday in the near room with her food and water and her favorite tattered blanket. All evening, whenever one of the hunters passed by the near room, she barked and scratched at the door.

The chess game began after dinner, and within a few moves, Erik knew he was a better player than Burdick, but he played slowly, deliberately making two sloppy moves to stretch out the game, hoping there would be less time for conversation. His hands were damp on the chess pieces.

Joseph and Alan were reading his magazines, inspecting his furniture, sitting in his chairs. Erik forced himself to sit and talk and smile, to act as if this were a normal evening on the Lone Sentinel, as if nothing were wrong and his father would be home soon.

"You *are* a fine player," Burdick said as Erik checkmated. He leaned back with his hands behind his head. "Your father had better watch out."

Erik smiled, saying nothing, and put the pieces back in their places.

"Is this your family, Erik?" Alan asked from across the room, pointing to the photograph that hung on the wall.

"My parents and I," Erik told him.

It was Erik's favorite photo. In it, Erik stood between his father and mother at the foot of the sentinel. His father was laughing, his mouth open and his head back. His mother's hand was on Erik's head, just curved over the top and touching his ear, smiling at her husband with amusement.

"I knew your mother before she lived here," Burdick said.

"Where?" Erik asked in surprise. He'd been ten when she died. More than anything, he remembered the sound of her laughter.

"She came to New Province for a year between her life at Triumph Sentinel and marrying your father. She was never really happy in New Province. I was sorry when I heard she died."

Burdick rocked onto the back legs of his chair. "Most young people on the sentinels live in New Province for a year while they decide how they'll spend their future." He narrowed his eyes, considering Erik. "You must be about ready for your year."

"I already know I want to stay on the Lone Sentinel," Erik said firmly.

"It can be a lonely life," Burdick said, holding up his hand before Erik could protest. "Oh, I know there are compensations. You're given the best foods, excellent medicines, a comfortable home. But on the other hand, there is the constant vigilance over the biosote, the risk of the aloneness. Your sentinel is especially remote. There's nothing beyond the Lone Sentinel except wilderness."

"Where will you go to hunt?" Erik asked, changing the subject.

Joseph, who sat in Erik's father's chair, laughed. "That's exactly what we've been trying to find out, young man. Burdick here claims to know the best hunting spot on the planet."

Burdick smiled. "You'll see. I'm not about to give away my secrets. I'll tell you this much, though. We'll travel another half day north and then angle to the east. Actually, we should be able to see your beam each night."

"Will you come back this way?" Erik asked.

Burdick shook his head. "No. We'll make a loop and rejoin the road about a day south of here. I want to be on our way tomorrow at first light."

Alan groaned, and Joseph chuckled. "Better tuck into bed, my son," he said.

When he'd shown the hunters where to sleep, Erik gratefully went to his own bedroom. His house felt ready to burst. He covered his head with his pillow and waited for the hunters to settle down and fall asleep.

Erik missed the weight of Thursday across the end of his bed. Worse, his thoughts wouldn't stop. He had barely trusted himself to speak to the hunters, afraid of what he might accidentally say. When the days were warmer, there would be more visitors to the Lone Sentinel. Not many, but each visit meant he might be found out, that he'd be forced to leave.

The beam slid overhead, and Erik tried counting the revolutions that lighted his room. It was no use; a glass of milk might help. He got out of bed and quietly padded to the kitchen in his bare feet, avoiding the living room where Burdick slept on a cot.

But as he entered the kitchen, Burdick sat up.

"Erik?"

"Yes?"

"Come sit down for a minute, would you?"

Erik hesitated, then made his way to the chair facing Burdick's cot. "I can't sleep," he said. "I thought I'd mix a glass of milk."

The pale night-light from the kitchen lit one side of Burdick's face. His hair stuck out in all directions as he propped himself on his elbows.

"I'd like to ask you something," he said. "You might think it's none of my business, but I hope you'll answer me truthfully."

"Yes?" Erik asked. Out the window, the beam passed over the biosote.

"Erik," Burdick said quietly. "Look at me."

Erik turned back to the rumpled hunter.

"Your father's not on Green Grass Ridge, is he?"

Erik didn't answer; he couldn't.

"Is he dead?"

Erik lowered his head. "He's dead," he whispered.

"Why don't you tell me what happened?"

The explanations, the lies, were gone. Nothing remained but the truth.

Burdick listened without interrupting while Erik told him everything, his words tumbling out in a disjointed rush at first, then more slowly, thoughtfully.

He described the fall, seeing in sickening detail the wind tearing his father from the sentinel. He told Burdick how he hadn't informed Trust Control so he could remain on the Lone Sentinel. He explained that he'd never varied from the demanding routine of the careman or let the beam go down, that he'd faithfully followed every rule in the Trust Operations Manual. He left out hearing his name called on the winter night when no one was there.

"I can't leave," he told Burdick at the end. "This has been my only home; I belong here."

Burdick turned his head toward the window. When the beam's light passed, Erik saw that he was frowning.

"Will you tell the Trust?" Erik asked.

"New Province is not a bad place to live, Erik," Burdick said, still looking out the window at the dark night. "There are people your own age, opportunities to learn, more recreation."

Erik said nothing. His stomach churned.

"You could take Thursday with you."

"Thursday hates strangers."

"You mean she hasn't had enough experience with strangers. She'd learn." He paused. "So would you."

"I don't want to."

Burdick sighed. "Your mother and father loved the life on the sentinels," he said. "I didn't have to spend a lot of time with them to see that. But they also knew the life at New Province. They *chose* to stay on the sentinels. They weren't hiding out."

"I'm not hiding out."

"I think you might be. You're not giving yourself the chance to choose between worlds. What you've done here by yourself has been brave, but you *are* alone. You need to consider the operation of the sentinel. What if . . . "

"Are you going to tell?" Erik demanded, cutting him off.

Burdick lay back down on the cot. "I'm not going to promise you I won't. I wish the decision could be yours, not mine."

Erik stood up. "I'm going back to bed. Good night."

"What about your glass of milk?"

"I've changed my mind."

When Erik got up in the morning, sticky-eyed from lack of sleep, the three hunters were already packing their gear into their vehicle.

"I slept like a baby last night, Erik," Alan told him. "The cots and tents that Burdick carries aren't a tenth as comfortable as your beds."

"We're *supposed* to be roughing it," Joseph said, combing his white beard with his fingers. "If you want a soft vacation, next year you'd better go to Bay Sentinel and lie on the beaches."

Burdick sat in the driver's seat, talking on the radio. Erik stepped closer to the vehicle. "Burdick clear," he heard him say.

Erik stood there until Burdick saw him.

"Erik," he said. "We appreciate the Lone Sentinel's hospitality."

"Were you talking to the Trust?" Erik asked.

"That's right. Telling them we're departing and all is well. Have to report in every morning and night, you know."

"Did you tell them all is well here at the Lone Sentinel, too?"

Burdick put his hand on Erik's shoulder.

"All *is* well, isn't it? While we're on this trip, I'm only concerned with hunting and keeping the Trust informed of our position."

The hunters climbed into their vehicle. Burdick leaned out his window and clasped Erik's hand.

"Take good care, Erik," he said.

"And you," Erik replied.

Long after the hunters were out of sight, Erik stood listening to the drone of their engine as it set off into the roadless north country. When he turned back to his house to let Thursday out of the near room, he could still hear the powerful vehicle pushing forward.

4
HAPPY
BIRTHDAY

It was a tinned cake, but Erik didn't care. There were tinned cakes in the supply room, as well as packaged cake mixes: chocolate, white, spice. He chose a chocolate cake and a can of chocolate frosting.

Licking the knife as he went, he frosted the cake in swirls and peaks, flourishing as he made the final peak stand up in the cake's center.

He counted out fifteen candles. The Trust thought of everything.

"Oh why not?" he said, and emptied all twenty-four candles from the box. He made a circle of candles around the edge of the frosted cake, then another smaller circle inside.

"What do you think, Thursday?" he asked, carrying the cake to the table and setting it in front of his usual place.

Thursday thumped her tail politely.

"Would you like a taste?" he asked and held out the frosting-covered knife to her.

Thursday stretched her neck and sniffed the knife, then pulled her head back.

"Chocolate doesn't suit you?"

He looked at the arranged place setting, his folded napkin. It would be easier to eat in the Reclina-Chair, even out of packages. Erik would rather eat that way now, but he didn't want to change any of the old routines.

"A careman is trusted to maintain his dignity and civilized state no matter what his situation," Erik's father had told Erik when he complained about cleaning up and preparing a meal and setting the table when they'd been in the midst of working on the sentinel's power packs.

If Erik continued to live the way he and his father had lived, maybe all of his life would stay the same.

"Since it's my birthday," Erik said aloud, "I decree that this dinner shall consist of birthday cake. Any part of it I want, as much as I want, even if it's only the frosting."

He struck a match and swiftly lit the candles, singing to himself as he worked the match from the center to the outer circle.

"Happy, happy birthday,
Happy, happy day,
Happy birthday, Erik,
Today is your day."

Thursday sat up with more interest as the candles caught and Erik sang. She cautiously set her chin on the edge of the table. When Erik didn't scold her, she wagged her tail, eyes bright on the burning candles. Erik leaned back from the flaming cake and commanded, "Make a wish."

His wish was hardly possible, Erik knew that. In one of the videos the Trust had sent, a video Erik had watched at least a dozen times, there was a vehicle, a sleek silver machine that sped along smooth roads Erik could only imagine. It squealed around the tightest corners and effortlessly glided up steep hills, shining like moonlight, a metallic magic.

The only vehicles Erik had ever seen were the heavy vehicles that carried hunters or visitors over the long, rough road to the Lone Sentinel or the lumbering half-track that Chad the supplier used to deliver the yearly supplies.

No vehicles were kept on any of the sentinels. "Trust Control doesn't want us to be tempted off the sentinels," Erik's father had explained.

"A true careman would never leave his sentinel unattended," Erik had replied.

"Well said, son."

The chocolate frosting hid the tinny taste of the cake. Erik gobbled the first piece, one-quarter of the cake. After the frosting on the second piece, the sugary sweetness stuck in his throat. He pushed the rest of the cake aside.

For once, in honor of his birthday, Erik left the table as it stood, with half-eaten cake on his plate and the rest of the cake sitting uncovered.

The video of last year's New Province Rally was already in the machine, ready to be played. The annual vehicle race wound through the hilly edges of New Province and ended in the center of the city.

A map of New Province was spread beside Erik's Reclina-Chair with the race course marked in yellow. A newspaper detailing the event was folded on top of the map.

As the Trust recommended, and as his father had done, Erik spaced out the newspapers in the supply room so that each day he took out the one that corresponded to the day's date, only one year old, never looking ahead to discover how an event turned out until it was the proper day to read about it.

Erik had asked his father why the Trust couldn't just as easily broadcast the news every day instead of making them wait a year to read it.

"We caremen have removed ourselves from the mainstream of New Province life so we can concentrate on the sentinels," his father had answered. "That's what's most important in our lives. The Trust doesn't want to cut us off from New Province events, only to remove their immediacy. A year's wait doesn't seem to make much difference, does it?"

Erik had to agree that no, it didn't matter that the news was a year old. It was like reading a book a chapter at a time, written long ago but still just as exciting.

The sugary birthday cake made Erik's head ache. After a glance through the window at the sentinel's beam smoothly rotating across the evening sky, he leaned back and closed his eyes. He'd take a short nap before he watched the New Province Rally video.

Minutes later he was wide awake and alert, gripping the arms of his chair.

Had the aloneness finally claimed him? He was sure he'd been roused by a pounding on the door of his house. The sound still echoed in the room.

Thursday slunk toward the door, the fur on her back standing straight up, her teeth bared. It wasn't his imagination, then.

The pounding came again: four raps, a pause, three raps. Insistent, demanding. Erik turned toward the tower of the Lone Sentinel, expecting to see the faces of dream monsters, but there was only the dark of night waiting for the beam to sweep past.

"Are you in there? Open the door. I'm freezing!"

Thursday snarled, circling in front of the door, her hackles up, her eyes wild.

Trust Control always notified the sentinels when visitors were scheduled to arrive. Colonists didn't leave New Province without notifying the Trust of their plans. Erik picked up the knife he'd used to cut his birthday cake and slipped it beneath his shirtsleeve with the cold point touching his wrist.

"Down, Thursday," he commanded. "Sit."

Thursday reluctantly edged back from the door and sat a few feet away, her hackles still up, ready to lunge.

The nights were still cold; maybe someone had become lost from a hunting party and was looking for shelter. He or she might be hurt. The voice, however, had sounded like a child's. Erik pulled the bolt on the door.

As the lock clicked, Erik realized he was acting against careman policy; he was endangering the Lone Sentinel. An emergency broadcast to Trust Control was the proper move *before* opening the door to a stranger.

Before he could relock the bolt, the door burst open and a small figure dressed in heavy clothing pushed in past Erik, followed by a rush of cold night air.

In the middle of the room, it stopped and turned around, stamping its feet and rubbing its arms.

"Close the door!" it commanded in its high voice.

Thursday leaned forward, growling. Erik motioned her still and shut the door.

Dark eyes snapped out from the figure's face. Its eyes were the only feature not covered. The creature was as tall as Erik's shoulder, and its clothing was muddy, with a splash of still-wet mud up one leg. A fur-lined hood covered its head.

"What are you staring at?" it demanded, pulling off one mitt and unwinding the gray scarf from its face.

Erik shrugged, unable to speak.

The figure dropped its scarf, and Erik saw its pinched features: a thin nose, dark eyes and arched eyebrows, high cheekbones and narrow cheeks, thin lips.

Wisps of dark brown hair showed from beneath its hood. The face looked young, but he couldn't tell whether it was a boy or a girl.

The figure rubbed its cheeks briskly with its thin hands, saying, "I can hardly feel myself. Do you think I've ruined my flesh?"

The figure was real, Erik told himself. Somehow this stranger had made its way to the Lone Sentinel and needed help.

There was a tapping at the window nearest the dining room table.

A face was pressed against the window, peering into the room. This other figure didn't wear a scarf, and Erik saw a face identical to the face of the figure standing before him: the same thin nose and high cheekbones, the same thin lips pressed together in a narrow line.

Erik stepped back. The figures couldn't be real! Not the same figure inside and outside. It had to be the aloneness. The knife in his shirtsleeve pricked his wrist, but what good was it against thin air?

"What are you?" he shouted roughly at the figure unzipping its jacket as calmly as if it were in its own home.

Thursday leaped forward, her fur jumping with electricity.

"Sit!" the figure commanded so self-assuredly that Thursday hesitated and sat back on her haunches.

"Don't be a fool," the figure said to Erik. "It's only my sister. She was lagging behind so I told her I'd leave her if she didn't hurry up." It paused. "I wouldn't have, though. I was only trying to scare her into hurrying. I thought we'd both freeze if we didn't move faster."

"Your sister?" Erik repeated, looking at the figure still standing against the window watching them. "But she . . . how can you be . . . she looks just like you."

"My twin sister," the figure said, shrugging off its jacket.

Under the heavy jacket, Erik saw what was unmistakably a girl's body.

"I'd better call her in," the girl said, "or she's likely to just stand out there. Wouldn't that be a fright to wake up to in the morning—somebody frozen to your window?"

The girl kicked off her muddy boots and walked in thick stockings to the door. Erik waited for the pile of clothes and the girl to disappear when she touched the door. A gust of wind in his imagination.

But the door opened easily under her hand.

"Willa! Come inside. It's warm in here, and he's all right."

The face at the window disappeared. The girl stood waiting in the open door with the cold air blowing an icy draft into the house.

"Come in, come in," the girl said impatiently, reaching out the door into the darkness.

In stepped the identical figure, her hood pushed back, showing the same dark brown hair. She stood just inside the door, looking down at the floor. Thursday tipped her head and perked her ears at this new figure. Her hackles smoothed.

"This is Willa, and I'm Augusta," the first girl said. She paused, looking expectantly at Erik.

"Oh," he said, "I'm Erik."

He tried to remember the polite thing to say when you greeted strangers, and finished lamely with, "Pleased to meet you, Willa, Augusta," nodding to each of them.

"Charmed," Augusta said, tossing her head.

"Charmed," Willa echoed in a soft, unsure voice, her head still bent toward the floor.

"Who are you?" Erik asked. "How did you get here?"

The girl named Willa cringed. "Is this wrong?" she asked her sister fearfully.

The other girl shot Erik an angry glance. He didn't repeat his question, but he couldn't see what had made her angry.

Augusta patted Willa's arm and said gently, "Let me help you take these clothes off before you overheat."

Erik stood by the table with his hand on Thursday's head and watched as Augusta's exact duplicate emerged from the heavy winter clothing. They each had short, dark hair, cut longer on the top and swept over their foreheads. Identical red wool sweaters and black pants, the same thick gray socks. They were the same height, the same slight size.

"Better?" Augusta asked Willa.

Willa lifted her head and smiled at Augusta. "Yes," she said, her voice barely audible. "Thank you."

Then Erik saw the difference between the two girls. Augusta's eyes snapped, taking in her surroundings in quick appraising flashes and narrow squints, barely considering one object before jumping to another.

But Willa's eyes were a dreamer's eyes. Her steady gaze didn't seem to reach the object in front of her, or maybe it went through it. There was a softness in her expression that Erik didn't understand.

Thursday stretched on the floor with her head on her paws, her eyes moving intently between Erik and the two girls.

"Look, Willa," Augusta said, leading Willa by the hand to Erik's table. "Erik has some nice cake for us to eat." She gave Erik a piercing glance. "Don't you, Erik?"

He hurriedly removed the piece of cake without frosting. It slipped from the plate onto the floor, scattering crumbs.

"Please," he said, bending down and scooping the cake back on the plate with his hands. "Let me get you each a plate. It's my birthday, and I was just eating the parts of the cake I wanted."

"How wasteful," Augusta said as she pulled out a chair for Willa.

"I was celebrating," Erik explained. "I don't usually waste food. Besides, there's plenty in . . . " He stopped. Why should he tell them there was a supply room full of food? Who were they?

He glanced at the Reclina-Chair in front of the video player, to see if he was still sleeping there and this was just a dream. But the big chair was empty.

Augusta raised her eyebrows when Erik slid the knife out of his shirtsleeve and used it to cut each of the girls a generous piece of cake. Willa ignored her fork and picked up the cake in her hands, jamming it into her mouth and swallowing in gulps. Chocolate frosting ringed her mouth.

Augusta held her fork in front of Willa. "This stuff is death on an empty stomach, Willa," she said. "You'd better slow down and use your fork."

Willa obediently set her cake on her plate and picked up her fork in chocolatey hands.

"Don't you have anything to drink?" Augusta asked as she speared a big piece of cake.

"Milk," Erik told her. "There's some milk already mixed up."

Augusta nodded, her mouth too full to answer.

Erik poured milk into two thick blue glasses. "How did you get here?" he asked.

"In Uncle Wayne's vehicle," Willa promptly answered.

Erik looked up in time to see Augusta shaking her head at Willa. "I didn't hear any vehicle," he said. "You couldn't get close to the sentinel without my hearing a vehicle. Is that the truth?"

Willa's eyes widened and she put her hand across the table to Augusta. Augusta took Willa's chocolatey hand and spoke to Erik in a careful, conversational tone, her eyes flashing.

"Don't you dare speak to Willa like that. *I* wouldn't have told you, but since she did, I can promise you that Willa never lies. *Never.*"

"Still," Erik said doubtfully. "I didn't hear. . . . "

"We didn't get this far," Augusta said, standing up. She led Willa to Erik's Reclina-Chair in front of the video player. "We bogged down in a muddy spot in the road quite a ways back. I was too tired and didn't see it. We had to leave the vehicle and walk." Augusta wrinkled her forehead. "It was farther than I thought."

"But Trust Control didn't announce that any visitors were on their way. No one leaves New Province without informing the Trust. It's the rule."

Augusta didn't answer. The two girls fit easily side by side in the Reclina-Chair. Augusta picked up the map of New Province and then the empty New Province Rally cartridge.

"Oh," she said. "This is *last* year's finale."

"*You* were driving the vehicle?" Erik asked.

"Of course," she replied. Holding up the cartridge,

she asked, "Do you want me to tell you who won?"

"No! I want to watch it for myself."

Augusta shrugged. "Suit yourself, but it's old news now."

Willa leaned her head against Augusta's shoulder. Augusta rocked a little, humming under her breath.

Erik sat opposite them, unable to take his eyes off their mirror images. Once, when Augusta closed her eyes as Willa fell asleep, he felt a cold shudder at the sight of their complete identicalness, no longer differentiated by even their eyes. He blinked. He'd seen only a few girls in his life, and he'd never seen twins. The summer before, a girl about Erik's age had stopped at the Lone Sentinel for a few hours with her father and brother. Erik had stayed in his room with Thursday until her party was gone.

Willa breathed evenly, sound asleep. Augusta gently moved her sister's head off her shoulder and leaned back to whisper, "Do you have a blanket?" She paused. "We're not going back out there tonight. Can we stay?"

Erik felt himself blushing. "Of course. You can sleep in my father's bedroom."

"Where is he?"

"Dead," he answered before he thought. Then he bit his lip.

"You're alone then," Augusta said, not sounding very surprised. "I didn't think caremen were allowed to stay alone on the sentinels."

"I'm a special case," Erik told her. He went on quickly before she could ask more. "I've never seen twins. You look identical, but your personalities are different. Are all twins like you?"

Augusta sat up taller on the edge of the chair. "What do you mean?" she asked.

Her response reminded Erik of the way Thursday's fur rose when she was angry. Was it rude to ask people such personal questions?

"I just meant that you're very different from one another, that's all."

"There's nothing wrong with Willa," Augusta said through her teeth, her eyes penetrating into Erik's.

"I didn't say there was," Erik said uncertainly, pressing back into his chair.

"Willa's fine," Augusta said firmly, shaking the hair from her face. "She's perfectly fine."

"I . . . " Erik began, but Augusta stood up.

"Would you please carry Willa to your father's bedroom? I don't want to wake her up."

Erik tried to lift the slight form of Willa from the Reclina-Chair without waking her. As he felt her warmth against him and her head resting against his chest, he knew he was blushing again.

"This *is* nice," Augusta said appreciatively when she saw his father's bedroom.

Erik glanced around the room in surprise. It was a simple room, nothing in comparison to some of the homes he'd seen in the videos and magazines. Augusta pulled back the covers, and Erik laid Willa on the bed as gently as he could.

When Augusta had covered Willa to her chin, she whispered, "Where can I wash up?"

Erik led her down the hall past his bedroom to the bathroom, conscious of her walking behind him in her stocking feet.

"There are towels in the cupboard," Erik told her as he switched on the light.

"Thanks," Augusta said, opening the cupboard and looking curiously at the folded and stacked towels and washcloths.

Erik watched as Augusta ran her hands over the towels and looked at the shampoo and soap on the top shelf, wondering if he should offer her anything more. She pulled a red towel and washcloth from the cupboard and said, "You're one of those 'everything in its place' people, aren't you?"

He couldn't tell her why he scrupulously followed every rule his father had kept, how keeping the Lone Sentinel in perfect order was like reciting a child's rhyme to keep safe in the night.

"Will you be returning to New Province in the morning?" Erik asked.

Augusta snorted. "We can't ever go back," she said, closing the cupboard with a bang. "We've run away."

5
AUGUSTA'S VEHICLE

While he waited for sleep, Erik puzzled over Augusta's announcement that she and Willa couldn't go back to New Province, that they'd run away. Had they run away *here,* to the Lone Sentinel?

As a careman, he was duty bound to extend hospitality to the two girls. And as a careman, he was also duty bound to inform Trust Control of their presence. Their parents in New Province must be looking for them, worried, afraid that their daughters were hurt or lost. What could Willa and Augusta have done that forced them to run away?

He was awakened by the smell of toasting bread. Thursday sat in front of his closed bedroom door sniffing the air while Erik pulled on his clothes.

"Come on, Thursday," he said as he opened the door. "Let's see what's happening now."

In the kitchen, Augusta was putting wrapped sandwiches and tinned drinks into Erik's rucksack, the one that usually hung in the near room.

Open containers of food and crumbs were scattered across the counter. The cupboard door was open above Augusta's head. Willa sat at the table eating a piece of toast and jam, humming to herself between bites. She waved her toast in Erik's direction as he entered the room.

"What are you doing?" he asked Augusta.

She jumped and spun around. "You startled me," she accused.

He started to apologize and then closed his mouth. It was his kitchen.

"I'm packing food to take with us," she told him over her shoulder, turning back to her preparations.

"You're going back to New Province, then?" Erik asked, unable to keep the relief from his voice. He'd offer her food from the supply room and help her pack it up. She could keep his rucksack.

Augusta shook her head. "No, we're not. I have to get the vehicle out of that mud. I think that between you and me we can have it free in just a few hours."

"I can't leave the Lone Sentinel," Erik told her.

Augusta stopped packing the rucksack and faced him. "Not even for a few hours? What could happen here?"

"Maybe nothing. Maybe the beam could go down. I can't take the risk."

Augusta put her hands on her hips. "I can't do it by myself. Nothing's going to happen if you leave for a couple of hours. Don't you have a radio you can carry so Willa could let you know if there's trouble here?"

Erik shook his head. "No radio. No vehicle of my own, and I can't leave, either. It's the rule."

"Rule? What rule? Whose rule?" She waved her hand into the distance, toward the south. "How will the Trust know? The chance that anything could go wrong is so remote it's not worth thinking about."

Erik shook his head again, not believing that she actually expected him to abandon the sentinel. "It's a chance I can't take. I'm sorry."

Augusta stamped her foot, and Willa stood up, leaving her toast on her plate.

"It's all right, Willa," Augusta said, smoothing her own face to blandness. "Sit down and eat now. Erik's going to help us get Uncle Wayne's vehicle out of the mud."

Willa smiled happily at Erik and went back to nibbling at her toast. Erik wondered if he were using the wrong words to talk to Augusta, words she somehow couldn't connect with what he meant. He tried again.

"I will not, because I cannot, leave the Lone Sentinel to help you with your vehicle. I can call Trust Control this morning and inform them of your predicament. They can have someone here the day after tomorrow to free your vehicle and take you back to New Province. Until then, I'll be happy to share my home and my food with you."

And if he called the Trust to tell them about Willa and Augusta, they'd know about Erik and his father, too. He pushed the thought away.

Augusta leaned her back against the counter, her shoulders slumping. She looked down at her stockinged feet.

"Then I'll do it myself," she said.

"The weather can still turn dangerous this time of year," Erik explained. "It would be better if you waited and let me call for help."

Augusta raised her head, her dark eyes wide and no longer angry. "Please don't tell the Trust that we're here. I promise we'll be gone as soon as we can, but they can't know we're here."

"Why?" Erik asked. "What have you done?"

"I . . . we haven't done anything that would make us criminals, if that's what you're worried about. Nothing that any caring, reasonable person wouldn't have done. I just think it's better if no one knows where we are for a while, until . . . "

"They wanted to take me. . . . " Willa began, standing at the end of the counter, her hands on her cheeks.

"Willa!" Augusta admonished. "Don't say anything else. Not now."

"I didn't mean to hurt the lady," Willa said, lowering her head. "I didn't want to go, Augusta."

"Oh, Willa," Augusta comforted her. "Don't cry. I promise they'll never take you away. You'll stay with me, and we'll see wonderful sights: beautiful mountains and strange birds and flowers. We'll have picnics and sleep in the grass under the stars." Augusta gripped Willa's shoulders and looked into her face. "It'll be fun, won't it?"

Willa nodded. "Will I have to take a bath every day?"

Augusta laughed. "Never, if you don't want to."

"But why the Lone Sentinel?" Erik asked. "Why did you decide to come here? It's remote, and there's nothing beyond here. Hardly anyone ever comes this far north except a few hunters."

"What place could be better? Who would think we'd be here?"

There was too much happening, too many emotions swarming in Erik's small house. He couldn't keep up with them all, and he felt as if there wasn't enough room to catch his breath. He had to leave.

"I have to inspect the sentinel before the Trust Broadcast," Erik told Augusta.

"Should I wait for you before I leave?" she asked, looking at him steadily.

"I've already explained my position here," Erik said. "I'm sorry."

Augusta snatched the rucksack off the counter, knocking over a box of cereal. There was nothing more Erik could say; he started for the door.

"You won't tell Trust Control," Augusta said after him. "Neither one of us wants the Trust to know the truth, do we?"

The menace in Augusta's words felt like a hand at Erik's throat. How could she know? He hurried out the door, nearly catching Thursday's tail as he swung the door closed behind him.

Climbing to the first level of the sentinel tower, Erik saw the heavily clothed figure of Augusta walking briskly toward the south, the dark blue of his rucksack bouncing against her back. Willa wasn't with her.

Beyond Augusta, seven or eight struckies flew in a clumsy flock outside the beam's reach. Any other time,

Erik would have enjoyed watching the birdlike animals.

At the third level of the sentinel, Erik sat and watched Augusta disappear into the hills. He had to have misunderstood her words; she'd almost sounded as if she were threatening him. She might guess, but surely it was impossible for her to know his true situation.

After his check was completed, Erik walked slowly back to the metal house, wondering what he could say to Willa. Strangers were bad enough, but Willa was even more mysterious than the usual stranger.

She sat on the living room floor, holding out her hand in the spring sunshine that slanted through the window, turning it slowly back and forth. The sun shone golden, highlighting the light hair on her arm. Thursday stretched on the floor, just out of her reach.

"I'm feeling the sun," Willa said. "It's very warm and beautiful, isn't it?"

Erik couldn't be sure she was really talking to him, but he nodded. "Would you like to watch a video or have something to eat?"

He was about to ask her if she'd like to read, but her dreamy face held him back.

"I can't," Willa said matter-of-factly. "Augusta said I should sit quietly and not bother you."

"It's no bother," Erik assured her.

"No, thank you."

Erik checked the kitchen counter and the table for a note from Augusta. In the near room, Willa's boots and jacket hung on pegs beside his own, but nothing of Augusta's remained.

* * *

"Anything to report, Lone Sentinel?" the voice from Trust Control asked during the daily broadcast. This was the moment for Erik to tell the Trust about Augusta and Willa. He paused.

"Report, Lone Sentinel," came the voice again.

"Nothing to report. Lone Sentinel clear."

"Trust Control clear."

Now Thursday lay with her head between her paws, inches from Willa's leg.

"Augusta went to get Uncle Wayne's vehicle," Willa volunteered. "She doesn't want it to be all muddy; she wants it to be clean."

"Doesn't Uncle Wayne need his vehicle?"

Willa turned her hand in the sunshine, making a fist and smiling.

"He doesn't know we have it. Augusta said it's a surprise."

"I have a feeling Uncle Wayne is very surprised," Erik muttered to himself on his way to the supply room for his newspaper.

In the supply room, he closed the door and sat on a box of tinned fruit and thought about Augusta and Willa, wishing he could stay in the supply room until they were gone. He wondered how badly Uncle Wayne's vehicle was stuck in the muddy spring runoff. His responsibility was to the Lone Sentinel first and last. If Augusta didn't return by dark, then he'd decide whether to inform Trust Control. It had been her decision to go after the vehicle alone, not his.

He scanned the row of videos and found one he thought Willa might like: *Summer Fun.*

Willa still sat in the sunshine, humming to herself

with her eyes closed, rocking back and forth in time with her humming. Goosebumps rose on Erik's arms. It seemed as if only her body was there. Too disturbing, especially when he wasn't used to any part of her being there.

"Willa," he said loudly. "I have a video. Would you watch it with me?"

Willa opened her eyes and frowned. "Augusta said . . . "

"It's *no* bother, Willa. *I* want to watch a video. You won't have to move a muscle; just stay right where you are and open your eyes."

"All right, Erik," Willa said. Thursday scooted a few inches closer to her, and she rested her hand on Thursday's head, barely pressing down on the fur.

Erik was reaching to turn on the video machine when Willa gasped.

"Augusta!" she screamed. "Watch out!"

Her eyes, those far-seeing, nonseeing eyes, were wide open, and her gentle face was twisted in terror. Thursday yelped and backed away from her.

"Oooh," Willa moaned in agony and held her right hand in front of her face. Erik dropped to the floor beside her as she gripped her wrist, staring at her hand in horror.

"She almost had it, but it slipped away and fell on her hand," she said, sobbing. "It hurts so much. Poor Augusta, my poor Augusta."

What was she talking about? Augusta?

"It's all right, Willa," Erik reassured her, clumsily patting her shoulder. "Augusta is fine. She'll be back soon."

Willa tilted her head back and looked into Erik's face. "Can you see her, too?" she asked.

Erik glanced uneasily around the house. "See her?" he asked. "What do you mean, see her?"

Willa wiped at the tears on her cheeks. "Augusta will be angry if she knows I told about it again. That's why . . . " She shook her head in quick jerks. "No. I can't tell that, either." She pounded her fists against her legs. "I can't tell anything. It's too hard to remember what I can talk about and what I can't. Augusta makes me promise, 'Don't tell anyone, never say a word,' but it's so hard to remember."

"What's Augusta doing now?" Erik asked.

Like a flick of the beam passing, Willa's face changed, going blank, withdrawing into herself. Her wet face calmed; her eyes peered above Erik's head as she smiled from afar.

"Augusta went to get Uncle Wayne's vehicle," she said sweetly to Erik. "Don't you remember?"

"But do you—can you—see her?"

Willa smiled, lacing her fingers together absently, turning them in and out as if she were playing the old birds-in-the-nest game he and his mother had played when he was just past babyhood.

Willa wasn't going to answer any more questions; maybe she didn't even hear him. Was this a special attribute of being a twin—knowing about each other when they were separated? He sat down, watching Willa, afraid to leave her by herself. Thursday crept back and lay down beside Willa with her nose against Willa's leg.

Erik shrugged away the thought that Augusta might really have hurt her hand. Another, worse, thought entered his head: What if Augusta had freed her vehicle from the mud and driven off, leaving Willa with Erik?

Willa wouldn't eat any lunch or dinner. She simply smiled politely and said, "No, thank you, Erik," when he offered.

It was dark when Thursday suddenly sat up and looked at Erik attentively. There was a pressure, like oncoming weather, a suggestion of movement and advancement, of air being pushed aside in unaccustomed currents and eddies. Erik put on his jacket and stepped out into the night.

There. He heard it: unmistakably an engine. Lighter than the hunters' vehicle, higher-pitched, faster. Then it was gone, taken by the light evening winds.

The night stretched starry above him. The beam smoothly turned across the sky, as much for Augusta's guidance, surely, as for the protection of the biosote. Erik took deep breaths. The air smelled of mud and of coming to life again. This had always been his favorite time of the year, when the dormant life came back and sweetened the days, when the insects swarmed and rushed to live out their short life spans before winter.

The sound took shape, vibrating in the darkness. He heard movement behind him and whirled around to face Willa.

"There she is! Oh, there she is! My Augusta!" Willa cried, pointing into the night, her eyes no longer focused far into herself.

A bar of lights bumped and jarred and swerved toward the Lone Sentinel at an alarming speed.

"Can she stop that thing?" Erik asked Willa.

Willa laughed happily. "Of course she can. Augusta is wonderful."

Erik wasn't so sure. He took Willa's arm and pulled her closer to the leg of the sentinel, ready to jump behind it for protection.

The lights grew larger; the engine buzzed and whined and groaned, pushed on by Augusta as she left the road and cut across the land toward the compound. Once the vehicle mired, then freed itself with spinning, catching wheels.

Quicker than seemed possible, the vehicle was in front of them, jerking to a stop by the still-open door of the house, illuminated by its light and the light from the beam.

This vehicle wasn't the sleek silver magic that Erik had wished for on his birthday candles. It was a rounded little vehicle, blue—maybe green—like a fat bug covered with mud. The windshield wrapped around the front so it blended in with the rest of the vehicle's ballish shape. Its tires were small and smooth, designed for the simple streets of New Province, not for uneven road and terrain. No wonder the vehicle had bogged down in the mud.

Willa pulled her arm free of Erik's hand and ran to pull open the driver's door.

"Oh, Augusta. You're back. I knew you could do it. I was so afraid when you hurt your hand, but I knew you could do it."

Augusta let Willa pull her out of the vehicle as if she were without muscles. She leaned against the vehicle while Willa hugged her, her arms awkwardly reaching around Willa, murmuring too low for Erik to hear.

Augusta's hair was matted. Wet dirt caked her clothes. One boot was gone, and her stocking hung off the end of her foot, heavy with mud.

"Let me help you inside," Erik said, reaching a hand toward Augusta.

Augusta lifted her mud-streaked face. "Don't you dare," she said hoarsely. "It's too late for your help now. I wouldn't have it for anything."

Erik stepped back from Augusta's anger; it boiled in the air around her like new storm clouds. Willa put one arm around Augusta's waist and one of Augusta's arms over her shoulder.

As Willa awkwardly guided Augusta past Erik, he saw that her hand was wrapped in a muddy cloth. In the light through the open door he realized that the mud was colored with Augusta's blood, which still dripped, sliding down her fingertips onto Willa's shoulder.

6
THE WOUND

Augusta was too weak to protest when Erik unwound the muddy cloth from her hand. She lay beneath the covers on his father's bed, her eyes half open.

Augusta's first finger twisted unnaturally toward her thumb where a deep gash began, stretching to her wrist. It was a more dangerous wound than Erik had ever cared for, filled with blood-soaked mud, surrounded by skin that had already turned an ugly red.

Erik filled a basin with warm water and pulled a chair next to the lamp beside the bed. Willa sat on the floor beside him, crooning, "Augusta, Augusta. My Augusta," whenever Augusta flinched.

Erik held Augusta's hand over the basin and washed the cut as gently as he could. It began to bleed again, turning the water in the basin bright red. Augusta kept her lips tight, her eyes squeezed closed.

The medical aid section of the Trust Operations Manual said that the most dangerous complication of any cut was infection. The manual recommended a colorless liquid antiseptic that was in the first-aid kit.

"This will help heal the cut," Erik said to Willa, showing her the clear bottle.

He folded a towel under Augusta's hand and poured the liquid directly from the bottle into the wound. Augusta screamed. She sat up in bed, knocking the bottle from Erik's hand, and then fell back in a faint.

Willa threw her arms around Thursday, her wide eyes moving from Erik to Augusta.

"I didn't mean to hurt her," Erik told Willa.

"It wasn't you; it was that," she said, pointing to the bottle of antiseptic on the floor. Erik let the antiseptic spill out darkly on the rug.

While Augusta lay in a faint, he set her twisted finger in a splint from the first-aid kit and wrapped it in soft gauze. With a heavier gauze he wrapped her hand until it looked like a lopsided ball.

Erik knew he'd have to inform Trust Control if the cut became badly infected. He didn't know how to do any more than he already had.

"It'll help Augusta if she sleeps," Erik whispered to Willa. "Why don't you sit in the living room with me until she wakes up?"

Willa edged closer to the bed. "I'm not leaving my Augusta," she said firmly.

"But she needs to sleep, Willa. She'll be fine in here."

Willa shook her head and put her hand on the bed next to Augusta's.

*   *   *

For two days, Augusta lay feverish, sleeping fitfully. Willa rarely left the bedroom, sleeping in a chair by the bed at night. Other than to change Augusta's bandages and give Willa directions, there was little Erik needed to do.

The two girls stayed in his father's bedroom, but Erik felt their presence wherever he went on the Lone Sentinel compound. He couldn't relax in his house, listening for their movements, wondering what he should be doing for them or what they might need. His time didn't feel like his own. When he couldn't see or hear them, he wondered if Augusta might be getting worse.

To try to put them out of his mind, Erik took long walks through the biosote fields and tossed Thursday's ball for her. He tinkered in the shed and stood outside watching for the borers and the struckies. He missed two days of lessons because his mind kept tripping over Augusta and Willa.

On the third morning, when Erik checked on Augusta, he found her sitting up in bed, her face pale and her eyes hollow, but without a fever. Willa sat cross-legged on the bed beside her, combing the tangles from Augusta's hair.

"I'll change the bandages on your hand," Erik told her.

Augusta didn't answer. She leaned against the pillows, wearing one of his father's shirts, her mouth a thin straight line.

"You look better this morning," he said, then coughed and rubbed his hands on his pants. "Your bandages *do* need to be changed. I won't take long."

Augusta turned her face toward Willa and held out her bandaged hand to Erik. The deep gash had pulled together. It was still edged with the redness of infection, but Erik was hopeful. He knew that the medicines provided to the caremen were the most powerful available.

"I think your hand's healing," Erik told Augusta. "You'll have to be careful with it for a few days, though, so your finger can heal."

Willa smiled in Erik's direction, humming the same monotonous tune.

Augusta took the comb from Willa's hand and set it on the bedside table. "I'd like to go sit in the living room," she said to Willa.

"I can help you," Erik offered.

Augusta looked at him coldly. "Willa can help me," she said.

Augusta was too unsteady for Willa's slight strength, but Erik stood back while they tottered their way to his father's Reclina-Chair. He told himself he'd jump forward if she needed help, but it would serve Augusta right if she stumbled.

Willa tucked a blanket around Augusta and sat on the arm of the chair, leaning her head close to her sister's.

In two or three days, if Augusta continued to improve, she and Willa could get into their little vehicle and drive back to New Province. Then the Lone Sentinel would be his again, his and Thursday's.

The morning breeze was soft and fragrant as he and Thursday did the daily check. The fresh green of the grass and low bushes finally signaled the true arrival of the short summer. The rains had tapered off, and soon the quick bright flowers would bloom before the stalks and leaves dried to golden brown.

On Green Grass Ridge, the fields of dusky pink biosote glowed like the sky just after a sunset. This was the time of year when the biosote on Green Grass Ridge was especially delicious to the borers and struckies.

After the check, Erik circled Augusta's muddy vehicle still parked in front of the door of the house. The mud had dried so thoroughly that it looked like a child's clay sculpture of a New Province vehicle. It wasn't even as tall as his chest.

"Hello, Erik."

Erik jumped away from the vehicle. Willa, dressed in her jacket and scarf, stood behind him.

"Augusta asked me to clean the mud off Uncle Wayne's vehicle," she said.

"I can help you, Willa," he offered.

"Augusta wants me to do it," Willa said, chewing on her thumbnail.

"But if we clean it together, it won't take us long at all. And then you can go back inside with Augusta."

And, Erik thought, it would be all set to drive back to New Province.

Erik put a water hose to the spigot and stretched it to the vehicle.

"We'll get the vehicle wet first, and the mud will come off easier," Erik explained to Willa. "There's an old broom just inside the door. Why don't you go get it, and we'll use it to loosen this mud."

Willa looked at Erik blankly, not moving.

"Inside the door . . . " Erik began again, then stopped and gave Willa the water hose. "You just get the vehicle wet, and I'll be right back."

Augusta was tucked into the Reclina-Chair with her eyes closed. But he suspected she'd just closed them when she saw it was Erik and not Willa entering the house. He grabbed the broom and left.

Willa diligently sprayed water on the vehicle. The mud loosened, running from the roof down the sides in rivers. Erik scrubbed at the vehicle with the broom, glancing every few seconds at the biosote fields, the beam, the perimeters of the Lone Sentinel compound.

The little vehicle slowly emerged from its shell of mud. It was blue, not the blue of the sky or water, but an artificial blue. A silly blue, Erik thought. Not a color you could look at and think, oh that reminds me of the sky on a summer day. But then the vehicle was silly itself. Its rounded shape and tiny smooth tires were as silly as its color.

Still, he reminded himself, it was a vehicle, a means of traveling at speeds he had never known. It had gotten Augusta and Willa all the way to the Lone Sentinel, so it must be a valiant vehicle. He patted its roof, as he might Thursday's head.

Looking through the clean windshield, Erik saw the mud-streaked blue seats and the small wheel for steering. There were only two gauges on the dashboard and two pedals on the floor. It was a very simple machine. A muddy boot lay on the floor of the front seat.

"Here's Augusta's other boot," he told Willa.

"I'll give it to her," Willa said, opening the driver's door.

"We should move the vehicle out of the way of the front door," Erik said. "Do you know how to drive?"

Willa nodded. "Augusta let me drive sometimes when the road was straight and flat, so she could sleep."

Willa sat in the driver's seat and pushed a button on the steering column. The engine whined and buzzed, and the whole vehicle vibrated. Erik directed Willa around the side of the house.

The vehicle lurched forward and then moved, slower than a walk, to the spot where Erik pointed.

Willa turned off the motor and opened the door. "Do you want to drive it?" she asked.

To drive. Even to drive this little vehicle . . . Erik pictured himself rounding the Lone Sentinel compound, becoming surer and surer of his skill until maybe he could take it up to Green Grass Ridge and look down at the land and the biosote fields and the sentinel.

He stopped. This was the danger of having vehicles on the sentinels: the temptation to leave for only a short while, to leave the sentinels unattended. It was what the Trust and the Helgatites foresaw when they banned vehicles.

"I guess not, Willa," Erik said, stepping regretfully away from the vehicle.

7
THE RADIO

During the Trust Broadcast, Augusta sat forward in the chair, cradling her injured hand.

"Lone Sentinel clear," Erik said at the end of the routine broadcast.

Augusta leaned back, pulling the blanket more snugly around her and settling deeper into the chair. Willa sat on the floor beside her combing Thursday, using the same comb she'd used on Augusta's hair.

Erik sat in the Reclina-Chair opposite Augusta and read his newspaper. After a few minutes of silence, Augusta asked, "Why do you even bother to read those old newspapers?"

"They're not old to me," Erik answered without putting aside the open paper.

"It doesn't make sense," Augusta continued. "The Helgatites and Trust Control set you out here in the middle of nowhere to watch a field of pink rocks so they can drop in every thirty years, and then they send you year-old news. What's the point?"

"The pink rocks are biosote, and the Helgatites return every ten years," Erik corrected her.

"Ten years or fifty years—so what? That story on the front page about the four children who disappeared? I can tell you how it came out, even though it's such old news most everybody's forgotten it by now."

"I'll find out in tomorrow's paper," Erik said.

"It's dumb," she muttered. "Living in the past where none of this exists." Then louder, she said, "They found all four of them hiding in an empty house, too afraid to go home for the trouble they'd get into."

Erik folded the paper in half and set it over the arm of his chair. "If you're so determined to tell me old news, why don't you tell me why you ran away from New Province in a stolen vehicle?"

Willa stopped combing Thursday and looked up at Augusta.

"Stolen?" she asked fearfully. "Did we steal? We didn't steal. That's not a good thing to do." She reached into the blanket and took Augusta's uninjured hand.

"Augusta wouldn't," she said with certainty, and returned to combing Thursday. Fur crackled with each stroke of the comb.

Augusta's eyes narrowed, and Erik thought she suddenly looked healthier.

"We had to," she said. "It was simply necessary."

She spoke in a conversational tone that Erik sensed she had developed to keep from alarming Willa. Unless she heard certain fearful words, Willa responded to tones of conversations more than their content.

"But what made it necessary?" Erik asked just as conversationally.

Augusta slouched in the chair and twisted the edge of the blanket.

"You might as well tell me," Erik said. "What did you do?"

Augusta's hair fell across her forehead as she bent over her hand. "They were going to take my twin to a place where there were others like her. For tests, they said, but I didn't believe them. We didn't know when. One day I was sent to the store, but before I got there, I felt something wrong. I came back just as it was happening." Augusta sank further under the blanket.

"Whoever made that decision?" Erik asked. He'd read about places that housed those unable to care for themselves. But Willa?

"The people we lived with. Our parents died in a vehicle accident when we were eleven. This is the third family we've lived with since then. Not all of them are happy with our . . . differences." Augusta nodded her head toward Willa. "She fought. When I tried to stop them, one of the attendants fell down the stairs."

"Was she . . . " Erik asked, not wanting to say the words *hurt* or *killed* aloud for Willa to hear.

Augusta shrugged. "I didn't wait to find out. We hid in a park overnight. In the morning, we went to Uncle Wayne's house. He was gone on another trip, but I knew where he kept the keys, so we took his vehicle and came here."

"But why here? There are no more roads to the

north beyond the Lone Sentinel. You can only go south, back to New Province."

"Uncle Wayne has a hunting camp a day from here," Augusta said, raising her chin. "We'll go there."

"A hunting camp?" Erik asked, remembering Burdick the hunter and his secret hunting spot. "Is your Uncle Wayne named Wayne Burdick?"

Augusta nodded.

"He told you about . . . the Lone Sentinel?"

Augusta shifted her eyes away from Erik. "Not exactly. When we took the vehicle, I took his maps and his notes from his last hunting trip, when he stopped here."

"What did they say?" Erik asked, tearing off a piece of the newspaper and rolling it into a ball between his fingers.

"That your father was dead and you were alone and hadn't told the Trust."

So Augusta hadn't been guessing that morning she left to free her vehicle. She had known he wouldn't want to call the attention of the Trust to his own situation.

"I won't tell the Trust about you," Augusta said.

"As long as *I* don't tell them about you," Erik finished.

"That's only fair. As soon as my hand heals, we'll go to Uncle Wayne's camp, and you'll never see us again. I know Uncle Wayne leaves supplies there, but maybe you can give us more. I'll pay you back someday."

"That's crazy. Your vehicle won't make it."

"We've got to try. I won't let them separate us."

"Suppose you did make it to the camp. Then what?"

"We'll stay until next spring. By then everyone will be so happy to see us again that they'll forget all this. They'll see that Willa and I can live together, and they'll leave us alone."

"But . . . "

"It's the only way," she said, setting her jaw stubbornly.

"You're wrong," Erik told her. "You've spent your whole life in New Province. You wouldn't last a week in the country beyond the Lone Sentinel. The only way is for you and Willa to go back to New Province."

"I'm so tired of sitting," Augusta complained, ignoring Erik, sighing and rolling her eyes upward. "If I could just smell some fresh air."

Willa clapped her hands. "You can see how clean Uncle Wayne's vehicle is," she said. "I'll get your boots. We found the other one in the vehicle, Augusta. I washed it."

When Willa had left the room, Erik said, "You can't continue on past the Lone Sentinel. There are no roads, nothing but wild animals and wilderness, no one to help you if you get into trouble. You have to go back to New Province."

"I won't talk about it," Augusta said, pushing the blanket onto the floor and sliding to the edge of the seat, gingerly holding her hand close to her body.

Erik heard Willa laughing in his father's bedroom. Thursday had followed after her.

"What *is* wrong with Willa?" he asked Augusta. "Why did they want to take her to that place?"

Augusta's eyes challenged Erik. "Nothing's wrong with Willa."

"But she *is* different from you."

Willa laughed again from the bedroom, and Augusta's eyes turned sad. "We used to be exactly alike. We could even trick our mother. But when we were ten . . . " Augusta paused and swallowed. "Willa fell off a tram bridge. She was in a coma for a week, and when she woke up, she was . . . like she is now." Augusta looked earnestly at Erik. "Sometimes twins can sense when something's wrong with their twin, but Willa *knows*, and if people find out, they get scared of us."

"Why did you live with strangers? Why not with your Uncle Wayne?"

"He's gone more than he's home. He makes his living guiding hunting parties and hikers. I'm not saying that the people we've lived with have been mean; they haven't at all. I knew long ago, when the first family didn't want us anymore, that someday Willa and I might be separated. I decided then we'd run away if anyone tried." Augusta looked earnestly at Erik. "She's fine, really."

Willa returned with Augusta's boots. Thursday tried to tug one of them from her hands.

At that moment, the radio suddenly signaled an incoming transmission.

Erik stood, forgetting Augusta and Willa. Thursday dropped the boot and barked. What could be wrong? Trust Control rarely made transmissions in the middle of the day, especially so soon after the daily broadcast.

"Lone Sentinel, acknowledge," said the Trust voice, followed by a burst of static.

"Lone Sentinel here," Erik reported. Another burst of interference filled the room as soon as he took his hand from the blue response button. He looked out the window at the clear blue sky—not a sign of a storm.

"Lone Sentinel, acknowledge," Trust Control requested again.

"What's wrong?" Augusta asked from the chair.

"Lone Sentinel here," Erik said again, louder.

"Poor transmission, Lone Sentinel."

The words were barely audible through the angry static. Erik turned up the squelch and said, "Strong interference. Is a later transmission advisable?"

"Negative." The radio crackled and spat. Erik could only make out the words, "important . . . identify . . . transmission . . . ites."

"Please repeat, Trust Control," Erik shouted into the radio. "Strong interference. Message unclear."

There was a sharp crack, like close lightning, and then silence.

"Acknowledge, Trust Control," Erik said into the radio, but the only sound was a gentle static.

"Trust Control, please acknowledge."

"Trust Control, acknowledge," he repeated. It was impossible for his transmission to be cut off! He pushed the blue response button again and again, futilely turning the fine-tuning knobs on the front of the radio.

"Acknowledge, Trust Control," he demanded, trying to calm his voice.

The radio remained still. But that couldn't be! It was his connection to Trust Control; he depended on it for his life.

Willa stood beside him, her hands over her mouth.

"What were they saying?" Augusta asked. "Do they know about us? Do they think we're here?"

Erik looked down at the pad of paper beside the radio where he'd jotted down the few words he could make out.

"The only words I could understand were 'important, identify, transmission, and something-ite,' " he told her. "Not much to go on."

"The word 'important' might signify something," she said tartly.

"Something," Erik acknowledged noncommitally. He looked up at the sentinel's beam crossing the clear sky. "It's only a temporary situation, I'm certain. It'll be transmitting properly by nightfall."

It had to be, he thought.

Throughout the rest of the day, Erik stayed close to the radio, calling Trust Control again and again, but the radio's continuous crackling never changed.

Instead of going outside, Willa and Augusta walked back and forth the length of the house several times. Each trip, Augusta leaned on Willa a little less. When they weren't walking, Augusta dozed and read in the Reclina-Chair, with Willa and Thursday sitting attentively beside her.

To pass the time, Erik tried to play dominos with Willa, but the dots confused her, and neither of them could keep their attention on the game. Willa's attention was on Augusta, and Erik's was on the radio. He avoided talking to Augusta as much as possible.

When it was dinner time, Willa wasn't hungry but Augusta was famished.

"I didn't think you'd ever ask me if I wanted to eat," she grumbled.

"But what about Willa?" he asked.

"Make enough so she can eat later," Augusta instructed.

All of Erik's routines were turned around. If Augusta knew how much she disrupted his life, Erik suspected she didn't care. With the radio down, his attention should be on the Lone Sentinel, not on trying to satisfy illegal guests.

"I'll fix a simple meal, then," Erik said.

He opened a cupboard and took out the worst foods he could think of: soy patties and dried mashed potatoes and a can of creamed corn. He banged the pans together in their cabinet until he found a little one for the creamed corn. He thought of dumping it all together in one big pot, like a dog's dinner.

"Lone Sentinel, acknowledge please."

It was a voice Erik didn't recognize. He left the can opener in the half-opened corn and rushed to the radio.

"Lone Sentinel here," he said, gratefully pushing the blue response button, laughing. His radio was back!

"Fourth condition, Lone Sentinel. This is Pod 56-H. Our expected arrival is ten-twenty tomorrow morning. Please refer to the sealed instructions in appendix C of the Trust Operations Manual and make proper preparations."

The voice was clearer than any Trust Control transmission. It could have been coming from the next room of Erik's house. Soft, almost melodic, the voice made sentences that flowed, one into the next, without stressing the hard sounds or syllables.

"Affirmative, Pod 56-H. Ten-twenty tomorrow morning. Preparations will be completed."

"Pod 56-H clear."

"Lone Sentinel clear."

As soon as the transmission was completed, Erik took a deep breath to calm himself and confidently called Trust Control. It was here: the moment he'd been trained for.

"Trust Control, please acknowledge."

But the radio responded with the same stubborn static as before the transmission. It was once again a useless black box.

Erik sat and stared at the radio. Somehow, there was interference between New Province and the Lone Sentinel. He lifted the Trust Operations Manual from the shelf by the radio. His father had been the last to open appendix C, when Erik was a baby.

"What is it?" Augusta demanded. "Who's coming tomorrow? Is it the Trust? Do they know we're here?"

Erik shook his head and removed the sealed envelope from the manual. He'd need a knife to break its seal.

"Not the Trust," he told Augusta. "The Helgatites will be here tomorrow."

8
PREPARATIONS

With a kitchen knife, Erik carefully slit the end of the envelope labeled appendix C. He read the first page of the instructions and stared helplessly at the radio.

The first order read, "CONTACT TRUST CONTROL IMMEDIATELY."

Unless the radio began working before morning, he wouldn't be able to comply before the Helgatites landed. The transmission problems had to be originating in New Province, not the Lone Sentinel, or his radio wouldn't have received the call from the Helgatites.

"The Helgatites!" Augusta exclaimed. "Aren't they a few years too soon?"

"That was what Trust Control was trying to tell me before the transmission broke up—that the Helgatites were coming. They must need more biosote sooner than their scheduled cycle."

"Why?" Augusta asked. "Do you think they had a disaster on their planet? From what I learned in school, the Helgatites aren't the type who'd be off in their calculations by a few years."

"I don't know. Only the Trust communicates with the Helgatites."

Augusta stood up and held out her injured hand. "Can I look at the papers?"

Erik stepped back, holding appendix C closer. "This information is intended only for the careman."

Augusta swayed a little on her feet. "I'm not about to tell anyone."

"Willa, help Augusta sit down again. She's not feeling well."

Willa jumped up and put her arm around Augusta's shoulders and guided her to the seat.

"Thank you, Willa," Augusta said, but not before she scowled at Erik.

"Willa, I'll be in my bedroom. Please call me if there's any sound at all from the radio."

"Yes, Erik," Willa said, sitting so she directly faced the radio. "I will."

In his bedroom, Erik turned on his light and stretched on the bed with appendix C. The orders were fairly simple. The beam's incline of rotation was to be raised to a tight eighty-four degrees and its speed lowered; the landing area must be cleared. The careman was to stand by the radio until landing was complete. He should supply the Helgatites with whatever their commander needed. While the Helgatites were operating at the Lone Sentinel, he was to give precedence to the Helgatites' needs or orders over Trust rules and customs.

There was more about customary greetings and proper protocol when conversing with the Helgatites.

Maybe he should let Augusta read *that* part, he mused, thinking of her snapping words and impatient eyes.

Erik read appendix C through twice and then read it through again, underlining passages with a pencil. There would be time in the morning to clear the landing area of any rocks and borer runs.

They were coming! He was going to see the Helgatites!

As he memorized the underlined portions of appendix C, Erik remembered that the runaway girls and the malfunctioning radio weren't his major problems. His father was dead, and it would be impossible to hide that fact from the Helgatites. It had been the Helgatites who'd first decreed that a sentinel be manned by at least two people.

Erik had broken two basic rules: He hadn't reported a death, and he was manning a sentinel by himself.

He rolled onto his back and stared at the ceiling. If he had to leave the Lone Sentinel . . . he couldn't do it. He wondered how well Burdick's hunting camp was built and how long it would take to walk the distance.

He knew his father could have handled the appearance of Willa and Augusta, and the radio interference, and the arrival of the Helgatites. Erik rolled back onto his stomach; maybe he wasn't ready to be a careman after all.

Every hour during the long night Erik got up and tried unsuccessfully to call Trust Control. Thursday followed him from bedroom to living room to bedroom, staying close beside him.

"This is one of our longest nights, isn't it?" he said to her once, stroking her broad head. He wondered if she really could adjust to living in New Province as Burdick had said she would. He couldn't see himself walking down a New Province street with Thursday on a leash, not ever.

Finally Erik dozed in the Reclina-Chair and dreamed of his father's fall, only in his dream it wasn't snowing; it was a clear spring day. His father fell slowly, so slowly that Erik knew he could catch him; there was plenty of time. Erik tried to move toward his falling father, but he could only stand heavy-legged and desperate, seeing his father slowly but assuredly descend to his death.

He jerked awake and opened his eyes. In the light of the beam, a figure stood in the hallway. His heart pounded. The shadowed light slid over, and the spooky shape turned into Willa. He started to say her name, but Willa turned and silently went back toward the bedroom.

Erik was awake before his alarm sounded. Aside from its continuous static, the radio was still as silent as the table on which it sat. In the kitchen, Augusta stood at the counter one-handedly fixing herself a bowl of cereal.

"Would you like some help?" Erik asked.

"No, thanks. I've got it."

"Where's Willa?"

"Still asleep. I think she's spent the last few days wide awake watching over me, so I thought I'd let her get some extra rest."

"She hardly left the bedroom."

Augusta nodded. She held up the cereal box in her

good hand. "Do you want me to leave this out for you?"

"I don't think I can eat anything this morning," Erik told her.

He held appendix C, intending to go over it once more before he began the day. The Helgatites . . . It wouldn't be long.

"I thought caremen ate according to a strict schedule," Augusta said, carrying her bowl to the table. "Go off your schedule, and the beam's liable to go down."

Erik couldn't tell if she were serious or taunting him, so he said nothing.

"Maybe if you ate breakfast properly, the radio would work again," she continued.

"There's a reason for every procedure and schedule that a careman follows," Erik told her.

"I'm only teasing. Do you always have to be so stiff? You even talk as if you learned by listening to those dumb *Say It Right* videos."

The *Say It Right* videos had been part of Erik's daily lessons since he was five. He sat in his chair and went over appendix C, trying to ignore the sounds of Augusta eating. He wondered if all New Province people ate so noisily.

"Lone Sentinel, acknowledge."

Erik recognized the alien voice he'd heard the night before. He took two deep breaths before he answered.

"Lone Sentinel here."

"This is Pod 56-H, Lone Sentinel. Our estimated arrival remains at ten-twenty. Please confirm preparations will be complete."

"Radio is malfunctioning, Pod 56-H. Trust Control

has not been contacted. All other preparations will be complete."

There was silence. Would the Helgatites decide not to land? If the Lone Sentinel was experiencing communication problems, would they choose another sentinel?

"We have informed Trust Control, Lone Sentinel. Your radio will be repaired after landing. Pod 56-H clear."

"They'll really be here in a couple of hours, won't they?" Augusta asked eagerly, almost smiling. "I've always dreamed of meeting a Helgatite. When we were little, Willa and I used to play at it. Sometimes she'd be the Helgatite coming to save me, and sometimes I'd be the Helgatite. Our mother even made us silver costumes."

"They'll have to be told of your situation here," Erik reminded her.

"What about *your* situation?" Augusta asked. "That will probably be more interesting to them than Willa's and my story."

"I'll explain my circumstances to them myself," Erik said, making his voice matter-of-fact, uncaring even. "But how will I explain your presence? I won't lie."

"Oh, I'm sure you won't," Augusta said and poured her remaining cereal down the kitchen sink. "What difference does it make to them? They're only coming to gather a little extra biosote; they won't be interested in two girls from New Province." She left her unrinsed bowl beside the sink and said, "Well, I intend to see the Helgatites *and* to meet them. You can tell them we're visitors from New Province. That's not a lie, is it?"

"Visitors are usually invited."

"Sometimes, where we live, they just drop in unannounced. That's all we did here on the Lone Sentinel."

Augusta always had an answer to whatever he said. It wasn't until hours later that Erik thought of what he *could* have said to her. He crossed his arms on his chest. "I thought you were hiding. If the Helgatites know you're here, whether they think you're my visitors or not, they'll probably relate the information to Trust Control. It would be easier to tell the Helgatites what happened to you and Willa in New Province. Maybe they could help you."

"I'm willing to take the chance that we're not important enough to the Helgatites to mention."

"You're much stronger today," Erik said. "You seem totally recovered."

"I'm better," Augusta said, narrowing her eyes.

"Your vehicle is ready to drive. Now might be the right time for you to start back to New Province. You must know that trying to live at your Uncle Wayne's hunting camp will be too hard for Willa. . . . "

"I won't take Willa back to New Province," Augusta interrupted.

Erik had to get his tools from the near room. He couldn't say any more to Augusta. She wouldn't listen anyway. The more he talked to her, the more confused she made him feel.

"I have to make preparations," he said.

Augusta eyed the appendix C still sitting beside his chair. Erik went back and picked it up.

"I'll take this with me," he said, folding it in half so it would fit in his jacket pocket.

Augusta sniffed and pulled her eyebrows together. She was always scowling and frowning. When he'd been sour as a child, his mother had said, "If you keep that up, your face will freeze in that position." Maybe Augusta's already had.

The morning was still edged with haze along Green Grass Ridge. The pink biosote fields had a delicate, dewy appearance.

Erik walked the length of the landing site, first its outer edges lengthwise, and then from corner to corner diagonally. The landing area was marked by a red block at each corner and a similar but smaller block every fifteen feet around its perimeter. The blocks contained a material that the Helgatites could lock their landing systems onto and use to guide their ship to exactly the right spot.

He crossed and recrossed the site, picking up rocks that were smaller than his fist and throwing them outside the area. He kicked small hills of dirt flat and shoveled heavy black earth into the hollowed-out spots.

"No, Thursday!" Erik had to keep saying when she tried to dig in the soft dirt he was moving.

Finally, Erik stood in the center of the landing site and leaned against his shovel. The site was as clear and smooth as he could make it.

In the shed beneath the sentinel, he raised and narrowed the beam to eighty-four degrees. He had often practiced the procedure with his father. He knew exactly which digital readouts were necessary, which buttons and levers to push. Only now he wasn't practicing.

Outside, the beam turned high in the sky, pointing nearly straight upward. As soon as the Helgatites landed, he would lower the beam again to protect the biosote.

Without the beam crossing above the compound, the air felt alien and empty, but with the change, the preparations were complete. Erik knew he had done them as well as his father would have. He and the Lone Sentinel were ready for the Helgatites, no matter what happened, no matter what the outcome.

Back in the house, he waited beside the radio at the accustomed time for the Trust Broadcast. But the radio was still dead. There was no transmission.

MAAG

Erik went through the motions of checking the supply room, standing unseeing in front of the full shelves. He picked up books and set them down again, opened and closed the cupboard doors. Always his attention returned to the window that faced the landing site and the sky above it. It wouldn't be long now, only a few more minutes.

Augusta and Willa sat together in the Reclina-Chair. Augusta was reading a simple animal story aloud, her voice droning tonelessly as she kept looking out the window and squinting at the sky.

The morning was clear and unclouded. They'd be able to see the aircraft as soon as it was in range. At ten-fifteen, Thursday started to whine and pace through the house, leaning first against Erik, then against Willa, pushing her nose into their hands and rubbing against them.

The sonorous voice came over the radio again, filling the room with its soft musical tones. "Request you stay by your radio until the landing is completed."

"Affirmative."

The metal house vibrated. Augusta took Willa's hand, her smile crooked. Erik clasped his hands behind his back and stood in front of the window, watching the sky.

First there was the sound, a humming similar to the workings of the Lone Sentinel's mechanisms, only louder. Much louder. Thursday tipped her head back and howled.

"It's all right, Thursday," Erik soothed.

A bright reflection flashed high above them.

"I think I see it," Erik said, pointing into the sky.

Augusta and Willa scrambled from the chair and stood beside him.

A silvery oblong glinted, smaller than Erik had expected. The oblong descended straight down, as if it were being lowered on a cleverly tied string.

The Helgatite ship vibrated the house like the winter wind. Its underside was smooth and unbroken, like a metal box. Willa and Augusta wrapped their arms around each other. Erik couldn't move, couldn't take his eyes from the ship's approach. It descended slowly, impossibly, like an apparition.

"What's keeping it up?" Willa whispered.

As it neared the ground, Erik made out what might be windows along the sides of the ship. The rectangular shapes were smooth and reflected the light. If the Helgatites were inspecting the Lone Sentinel, they couldn't be seen.

"It seems too small to carry enough biosote to last ten more years," Augusta said.

Erik agreed. The oblong ship wasn't even as large as his house. It filled only one corner of the landing site as it set down; its humming turned higher-pitched, then abruptly cut off.

Thursday lunged at the window, barking and growling at the strange machine. Erik wouldn't have touched her when she was so angry, but Willa put her hand on the dog's back. Erik jumped forward, but when Thursday saw it was Willa, she immediately calmed down.

"Lone Sentinel. This is Pod 56-H. Please acknowledge and attend our entry."

"Lone Sentinel acknowledges, Pod 56-H. I will attend."

In front of the mirror above the radio, Erik smoothed his hair and straightened his shirt collar.

"I want to come with you," Augusta said from behind Erik, her face reflecting in the mirror.

"It's not permitted, Augusta," he explained. "You're not an official inhabitant of the Lone Sentinel. It wouldn't be proper. You can watch from the window."

"I could just stand outside the door."

"Please stay inside."

"Please stay inside," Augusta mimicked, disappearing from the mirror.

Erik stepped out into the balmy day. He thought of how his father must have felt years ago when he'd greeted the Helgatites in exactly the same way that Erik would. The same way that all caremen greeted the Helgatites.

The ship sat flat on the landing site, only about ten feet tall. Its oblong shape, rounded at the corners and edges, was like a silver bread loaf. The rectangles that Erik thought were windows looked just as blank close up.

The largest rectangle smoothly and silently opened, sliding back to reveal a set of steps that ended a few inches above the ground. Erik waited, his shoulders back and his head held upright.

A figure glided down the steps. Its head was covered by a narrow bubbled helmet. A suit of silvery fabric, duller than the pod, covered its entire body, ending in silver gloves and boots.

The alien figure was like those Erik remembered seeing out the window years before. But now, here it was, right in front of him: a Helgatite.

Appendix C said the Helgatites were not to be touched for any reason. Erik stepped back, bowing formally.

"You are welcome to the Lone Sentinel," he said.

"Thank you, Careman," the figure answered in the same modulated voice that had broadcast over the radio. It raised its hand in greeting and stepped—flowed—closer to Erik.

The Helgatite was thinner than Erik, even in its protective suit. Erik had to tip his head back to look at the helmeted head. His helmet was as blank as the pod's windows. Erik couldn't make out any features.

"I am Maag. I will be the liaison between you and our group. We will be here only a few days. Our pod will provide the food and resting place we need. You may continue your life on the Lone Sentinel as normal."

As normal? How could life on the Lone Sentinel be normal when the Helgatites were there?

"I am honored, Maag. I am Erik of the Lone Sentinel. If I can assist in the gathering of the biosote as my father did before me and his father before him, I would be honored even more."

"There will be no gathering on this journey, Careman Erik. We are here to apply a solution that encourages faster growth of the biosote. It is advised that you stay away from the biosote fields when we work. The solution has not been tested for its effects on your species. It could be harmful."

Appendix C made it clear that the orders of the Helgatites were not to be questioned by the caremen: They were to be followed implicitly.

"Thank you for the warning, Maag. While you are here, all that is mine is yours."

"You are a gracious host," Maag replied. "You may also return the beam to its normal rotation."

Maag raised an arm loosely toward the pod. Erik tried to see inside without being obvious, but only the steps were visible.

"We will make preparations now, Careman Erik. Do not risk contamination from the solution."

Erik bowed and turned to leave.

"Careman Erik?" Maag said.

"Yes, Maag," Erik answered, turning back.

"Where are the others of your careman family?"

It was the question he knew had to come. He couldn't lie to a Helgatite.

"There are two guests here from New Province," he said. "And my dog. My father died in a fall four months ago."

Except for the light breezes, the day was totally quiet. Even the raucous rock birds had been silenced by the alien ship's descent.

Maag finally asked, "You have been manning the Lone Sentinel alone?" There was no emotion in his voice, no hint of approval or disapproval.

"Yes, Maag. The beam has never faltered."

Again Maag paused. Erik waited. How quickly would the Helgatite decide his fate?

"This is an unusual situation, Careman Erik. It will be considered."

"Thank you, Maag," he said, unsure of Maag's meaning. He felt a sudden hope that the Helgatites might want to judge him by how well he handled their visit to the Lone Sentinel. He'd make sure their stay went perfectly.

"We know that your radio is not operating properly. We will repair it for you before we leave. Have you attempted your auxiliary radio?"

The auxiliary, in the supply room. In the confusion with Willa and Augusta, he'd forgotten it. It was no excuse. He closed his eyes in embarrassment.

"Perhaps you should try it now," Maag said softly.

Erik nodded and bowed again. As he returned to his house, he looked back at the tall figure of Maag standing so still beside Pod 56-H.

Erik opened his door wide, his mind on the Helgatites and the radio in the supply room, not on danger that might come from his house.

Thursday leaped past him, barking furiously, knocking Erik off his feet. Willa screamed.

"Thursday!" Erik shouted.

Thursday's furred muscles rippled as she raced on toward the Helgatite ship. Maag stood beside the open door of his ship, facing Thursday's approach.

"Thursday!" Erik shouted again.

Erik jumped to his feet. Thursday was his responsibility. It was as if Erik himself were attacking the Helgatites.

Maag stood perfectly still, watching Thursday as she ran directly at him, her head low and her mouth open.

"Get inside!" Erik shouted to Maag.

As Thursday sprang, Maag calmly raised his gloved hand. Thursday dropped in midlunge, falling in a heap at Maag's feet, lying still.

"No!" Willa cried out and shoved past Erik.

Erik and Augusta ran after her. Erik hadn't thought Willa could run so fast. Her dark hair fluffed back like wings as she raced toward the pod. Erik caught up with her only a few feet from Maag.

"You hurt her. You hurt her," she accused Maag.

Erik held Willa by the shoulders as she struggled to reach Maag, her usually dreamy face twisted in anger.

"Let me," Augusta said behind him, and Erik released Willa into her arms.

"I apologize," Erik told Maag. "Thursday, the dog, is very important. She is a companion."

"You're bad," Willa said to Maag. "You hurt Thursday."

"You must practice more control over your companion, Careman Erik," the Helgatite said in his soothing voice.

"Have you killed her?" Augusta demanded.

"She is not hurt," Maag said. "She might have damaged my suit. She'll be fully operative soon. I suggest, Careman Erik, that you take precautions to have your companion under restraint when she arouses."

"I'll get her leash from the house," Erik said. Thursday wasn't hurt, but for a horrible instant Erik had thought he'd lost Thursday, too.

He motioned for Augusta to bring Willa and come with him, but she looked away and spoke quietly to Willa.

The heavily woven leash hung on the wall of the near room next to his jacket. Erik jammed the leash into his pocket and rushed out of the house.

Augusta stood in front of Maag with her hands on her hips. Erik hurried, lengthening his stride. Willa sat beside Thursday, stroking her head. Whatever Augusta and Maag had been discussing was finished by the time Erik reached them. Augusta's back was to Maag, and her face was red.

"I'll take better care in the future," Erik said as he put the restraint on Thursday. Thursday groggily pawed at Erik's hands, whimpering.

"I'm sure you will, Careman Erik. Caution is learned from inattentiveness." Erik and Maag bowed formally to each other again, and Maag gracefully ascended the steps of Pod 56-H.

Thursday came to life. She snapped angrily at the unaccustomed leash. Erik wrapped the loop around his wrist while Willa crooned and petted her until Thursday was willing to slink along between them. She tugged experimentally on the leash every few feet.

"What were you talking to Maag about?" Erik asked Augusta.

"Oh, is that his name?" she asked.

Erik waited for her to answer. She brushed at her hair with her hand.

"I asked him to fix Willa," she said.

Erik stopped, jerking on Thursday's leash. "You what?" he asked incredulously.

Thursday sat down on her haunches at the jerk, and Willa frowned at Erik and Augusta.

"Let's all walk together to the house," Augusta said conversationally. "I think Thursday likes to walk with you best, Willa. Maybe Erik would let you take her leash."

"It's too dangerous," he said. Then, seeing Willa's disappointment, he added, "But would you help me keep her calm?"

"Of course, Erik," Willa agreed happily, turning her attention to Thursday.

"Why did you ask Maag to do that?" Erik asked Augusta.

Augusta raised her chin. "Everybody says the Helgatites are gifted in the repair of humans, that they know medical techniques for diseases we aren't even advanced enough to have. How much trouble would it be to fix one girl? They could do it in an afternoon." She snapped her fingers. "Like that."

"What did Maag say?"

Augusta tossed her head. "Garbage about Nature making her own best decisions, that he couldn't interfere with the course of our lives. Nothing as kind as I'd heard the Helgatites were supposed to be."

"You broke protocol to ask a Helgatite a direct question," Erik told her. "You have to follow the customs."

"And how am I supposed to know the customs or the 'protocol' if you won't let me read about the proper way to approach a Helgatite?"

"You should have left it to me. It's what I'm trained for; it's part of my life as a careman."

"Oh, I'm sick of you and your silly careman's life and all your stupid rules. Do this now. Do that next. Everything has to be in proper order. Don't think for yourself. All I know is that if all the Helgatites are like your pal Maag, we're lucky they only show up once every ten years."

10
THE SOLUTION

"I've only seen nine Helgatites," Augusta said from the Reclina-Chairs where she and Willa had settled to watch the Helgatites and Pod 56-H.

Erik paused on his way to the supply room and looked out the window. "Including Maag, you mean?" he asked.

Augusta nodded. "Your dear Maag seems to be in the thick of the whole works, doesn't he?"

Erik thought so, too. He'd watched the Helgatites leave Pod 56-H carrying the containers of solution that stimulated the biosote growth. They all wore the same pale silver suits with bubbled headpieces, but there was no mistaking Maag's air of command, the confident way he moved among the others, or the way the other Helgatites deferred to him. Erik wasn't sure, but Maag also seemed taller than the other Helgatites, and more agile.

"Do you think there are more inside?" Augusta asked. "Standing guard in case we try to sneak in and put our grubby hands on their precious machinery?"

Erik shrugged. He'd wondered the same thing.

By now the Helgatites had entered the biosote fields below Green Grass Ridge. Every few feet they stopped and sprayed their solution from nozzles. The containers were small, hardly bigger than the pitcher Erik used for milk. He thought he could easily carry a container ten times that size, but the Helgatites bent under their weight and had to set them on the ground between each spraying.

"How long is all this spraying supposed to take?" Augusta asked.

"They didn't say exactly. Only a few days."

"Do you think they're prepared in case there's an accident—say one of them drops a container of solution on his foot or trips over a rock?"

"They wouldn't come this distance without being prepared for any possible accident," Erik told her.

He wished she'd stop talking about the Helgatites. She seemed to think they were ordinary, or worse yet, a joke.

"I have to check the auxiliary radio," Erik said. "Come, Thursday."

Willa put her hand on Thursday's head. "I won't let her chase the intruders again, Erik."

"I know you won't, Willa," Erik assured her, "but I've decided to keep Thursday with me while the Helgatites are here. She's too strong for you."

While he pulled the auxiliary radio from the back of its shelf, Erik wondered why Willa had decided the

Helgatites were intruders. Was it a word she "saw" in Augusta's mind?

The auxiliary radio was smaller and simpler than the regular radio. Erik set it on a sorting table and removed its dust cover. It was already set to the Trust Control frequency. When he turned it on, the dials lit up pale yellow, but the same low static sounded from it.

He pushed the response button anyway and said, "Trust Control, this is the Lone Sentinel. Please acknowledge."

There was no answer. Erik tried again, but he heard only soft interference. His hopes fell. What if New Province was gone, just like Earth?

A timid knocking sounded on the supply room door. Thursday sat up and wagged her tail.

Willa stood in the doorway, clasping and unclasping her hands in front of her.

"Erik," she whispered. "I don't think Augusta should have gone."

"Gone where?"

Willa waved her hand vaguely behind her. "Out there."

The Helgatites! Augusta had waited until he was out of the room and then gone to confront the Helgatites again. He was sure of it.

"Willa," Erik explained slowly. "I'll go outside and bring Augusta back, but I'll have to leave Thursday with you. Can you take care of her?"

Willa held out her hand to Thursday. "Of course I can."

Erik fastened Thursday's leash to her collar and tied

the other end to the heavy leg of a Reclina-Chair. Through the window he could see Augusta beside Pod 56-H.

Erik securely closed the door of the house behind him. Now that he knew where the door of Pod 56-H was, he easily detected its outline, even closed. Augusta was bent over, peering at the door. He heard her questioning, "Hello?"

From the biosote fields, Maag moved rapidly toward Augusta, seeming to skim above the ground. Augusta's bandaged hand reached toward the skin of the Helgatite ship.

"Augusta!" Erik called.

Augusta jerked her hand away and whirled toward Erik, her eyes bright, challenging. Erik braced himself for a quarrel.

"You mustn't touch the pod, Augusta," came Maag's melodious voice.

"Why not?" Augusta demanded, turning from Erik to Maag. "Will you punish me?"

"Of course not," Maag said. "The pod, like all our ships, has an automatic protective field that is implemented when the door is closed. It would not harm you, but it could cause pain." Maag bowed his helmeted head. "And we wish to cause no pain."

"Can we go inside?" Augusta asked.

"I would very much like to show you the inside, but our body differences make it impossible. This pod is much too fragile, but should you be here when the major ship lands, it would be an honor to give you a tour."

Maag bowed to Erik. "And you, too, Careman Erik."

"The major ship?" Augusta asked, stepping close enough to Maag to touch him. "When is the major ship coming?"

"Not at this time," Maag said, his voice still pleasant and courteous. If he was feeling impatient with Augusta, it didn't show.

Augusta was breaking every rule that the Helgatites had established in the Trust Operations Manual. She had confronted them, questioned them, and attempted trespass. Erik had to get her away before she did anything else.

"Willa is waiting for us inside, Augusta," Erik told her.

"Willa," Augusta said to Maag, her voice rising. "My sister Willa. You could help. . . . "

"We must go now," Erik said firmly and took Augusta's arm. Augusta tried to shrug him free, but Erik tightened his grip. Maag stood silently, watching, and Erik wished he could see Maag's face, even just his eyes.

"We take leave of you, Maag," Erik said, bowing, and forcing Augusta to bow with him.

"Until later, Careman Erik, Augusta," Maag returned, bowing.

Erik pulled Augusta along beside him, his hand tight on her arm.

"You're hurting me," Augusta said through her clenched teeth.

"Just come with me," Erik whispered back.

"Let go. I promise I'll go back to the house with you," Augusta said, stiffening her legs and bringing them both to a stop.

"All right," he said, releasing her arm, "but remember, you promised."

When he was sure Maag wouldn't hear, Erik said, "Augusta, we owe our lives to the Helgatites."

"I know, I know," Augusta grumbled. "I got an A on that quiz, and I wrote an essay called 'Our Debt to the Helgatites' that was read in front of the whole school. I know all that ancient history."

"Then you should understand that *I* have to be the contact with the Helgatites. We have to treat them as our guests and benefactors, exactly as they deserve."

"But that was school. This is real. The Helgatites can fix Willa. They can help us *now.*"

Erik didn't answer. All his life he'd been in training to meet the Helgatites. It was the reason he and his father had maintained the Lone Sentinel. And in a way, it was the reason his father had died. Now, what he did, how well he managed, could determine his whole future. He couldn't let Augusta destroy all he'd worked and hoped for. It was understandable that the Helgatites couldn't tend to Willa right now.

"Oh, Augusta," Willa said, smiling and clapping her hands when they entered the house. "I'm so happy to see you."

Erik untied Thursday. Before he went back to the supply room he stopped hesitantly beside Augusta.

"Quit worrying," she snapped. "I'm not going out to bother your precious Helgatites again."

He called Trust Control, two, three, then four times without a response. Finally, he re-covered the radio; it was useless to try any more.

"I want to look through the newspapers." Augusta leaned over the stack of wrapped New Province newspapers, already lifting the top one.

"Put it back," Erik told her.

"I'm not going to hurt them. I just want to find an article I remember."

"I don't read ahead," Erik told her. "I read one paper every day."

"But it's important," Augusta said, unwrapping the first paper. "I can't remember exactly what it said, but it was about the Helgatites. . . . "

"No," Erik said wearily. He took the newspaper from her and put it back on the stack. "Stop interfering with careman procedures. I read one paper every day."

"You're not listening to me!"

"You're the one who's not listening. In less than two hours you've broken nearly every rule the Helgatites set up with Trust Control. You may have done damage that could last for generations."

"But don't you see—they could fix Willa! The Helgatites could make her the way she was before she fell. It would be nothing to them, but it could mean everything to Willa."

"You mean everything to *you,* don't you?" Erik asked, lowering his voice. "Willa's happy with the way she is. Besides, if you'd give the Helgatites time, they might decide on their own to help Willa. Demanding isn't the way to approach the Helgatites. You're doing it all wrong."

Augusta pounded her fist on the nearest shelf. "You think everything I do is wrong, but you won't tell me how to do it right. It's all a precious careman secret to you. What does any of this," Augusta swept her hand in a circle, taking in the entire Lone Sentinel compound, "matter compared to Willa? It's just a thing, a place. Willa's real. She's my sister."

"To the Helgatites, *this* is everything. They couldn't live without the biosote. Let them take care of that first."

Though the supply room was cool, Augusta's forehead was damp with perspiration. She looked at Erik with wide eyes.

"Don't you see?" she whispered. "It was my fault. They have to help Willa."

"What was your fault?"

Augusta bent her head. Her hands shook.

"She was sick. She was supposed to stay home in bed, but I teased her into coming with me. I told her she was a baby if she didn't climb up the tram trestle with me. She said she was dizzy, but I wouldn't listen; I called her a coward. And then she fell. . . . "

Augusta covered her face. Erik didn't know what to do. The supply room closed in on him; it was hard to breathe.

"Augusta," he said, unsure.

Augusta pulled her hands away from her face. "Go away," she said angrily. "Leave me alone. There's nothing you care about but your stupid sentinel."

"But, Augusta . . . "

She stamped her foot. "Go away!"

Augusta leaned her head against the shelves. She'd told him to go away, but somehow she didn't sound as if she wanted to be left alone. He reached his hand toward her and then put it in his pocket.

"I'm going outside for a while," he finally told her.

"Go ahead. Just run away from it," Augusta said, keeping her head averted.

It was too much. He was sorry she felt responsible for Willa's injury, but he couldn't cure Willa. And procedures had to be followed.

"Where are you going, Erik?" Willa asked as he fastened Thursday's leash to her collar.

"I'm taking Thursday for a walk. You wait here."

Outside, the beam circled above them, its arc rising and falling across the sky above the biosote, up and down, as steady as ever. Thursday growled and strained on her leash when she saw the pod.

There were no Helgatites in the biosote fields. Erik assumed they were inside the pod, eating or resting or whatever they did between their episodes of spraying the biosote.

He led Thursday toward the edge of the compound, pondering his problems—first Willa and Augusta, then the Helgatites. How could he repair everything that had gone wrong? The radio, Augusta's confrontation with Maag, his own deception of Trust Control. All he'd learned over the years seemed useless.

Thursday tugged on her leash again, and Erik looked around in surprise. Without realizing it, he'd walked into the biosote field where the Helgatites had been spraying.

Erik had grown up with biosote; he'd studied its cycles. He knew the pale pink bloom that came every spring and hardened over the summer into rocklike filigree. He was familiar with its long, slow, barely perceptible growth.

But this wasn't right. The new pink was shriveled and black. Even the darker red of the older biosote was black. It looked dead. He knelt and touched the low blackened growth. It crumbled in his hand.

Thursday growled low in her throat, and Erik looked up.

Making his floaty, shimmery way toward Erik and Thursday was Maag.

11
THE POD'S SECRET

"Careman Erik, it is best for you to avoid this area. There may be danger to your humankind from the growth solution."

Thursday slunk down on her belly beside Erik, her ears back and her eyes riveted on Maag.

"I was deep in thought, Maag, and wasn't watching where I walked. Thank you for reminding me."

Erik waved his hand around him at the blackened biosote.

"The biosote . . . " he said, then stopped. He'd been about to ask Maag to explain the biosote's condition. Was he getting to be like Augusta from listening too long to her meddling ways?

Maag didn't seem to mind. His voice chimed, like laughter. "You're wondering why the biosote looks the way it does," he said, "almost as if it were dead."

Erik nodded.

"I know. That was my impression when I first saw the effects of the solution, that we'd destroyed our means of life. But it is only the appearance. The solution arrests the growth for a short while until it takes hold. Then the biosote blooms and produces three years' growth in only one season. In a week, you'll see the growth begin, and then it will be safe for you to walk in the biosote fields."

"I'm relieved by your explanations," Erik said gravely. He felt a crawly sensation as if he were being closely scrutinized.

"Your radio is still inoperative?" Maag asked.

"The auxiliary radio doesn't work either," Erik told him.

"This planet you call Azure has had a series of magnetic storms this season. Since we've landed our communications have been too disturbed to transmit properly. If the radio transmissions aren't restored by our departure time tomorrow, we will investigate more thoroughly."

"The spraying will be completed tomorrow, then," Erik said, trying not to sound as if he were questioning Maag. He could see that less than a quarter of the biosote had been sprayed. Those sections of the fields lay blackened, as if they'd been burned.

"We will be finished tomorrow afternoon," Maag said. "Your atmosphere tires us out, and we cannot accomplish very much this first day. We will rest the remainder of the day and replenish ourselves. Tomorrow our fatigue will be much less."

To the west, dark clouds with dense gray edges

gathered along the horizon. The breeze felt damp and cool; it would probably rain soon.

"Careman Erik," Maag said. "You should leave this area now."

Erik looked up at the helmeted head. His own distorted reflection shone back at him. "Thank you," Erik said and bowed. "I take leave of you."

Maag returned his bow, and Erik started down toward the Lone Sentinel. The silver Helgatite Pod 56-H glinted against the spring greens. The nose of Augusta's bright blue vehicle stuck out from behind the corner of the house. Silver and blue, like two rare jewels in the midst of drab and green.

If Erik could keep Augusta and Thursday away from Maag, there was still a chance that the encounter with the Helgatites could end successfully. Maag would see that Erik was mature enough to be the Lone Sentinel's careman. He would tell Trust Control that the rules should be relaxed in Erik's case, just this once, and Erik and Thursday could stay on the Lone Sentinel. Even living on the Lone Sentinel with a replacement careman would be better than being banished to the noise and crowds of New Province.

Erik glanced back at Maag heading farther into the biosote, walking in that gait that seemed to barely hold him to the ground, leaning now and then to inspect the blackened growth.

What harm could it do if Erik were merely to walk around the pod, to study but not touch it? It would take only a few seconds.

There was no sign or sound of any of the other

Helgatites who were "replenishing." Maag had left the door of the pod partially open, showing the extended steps. Erik didn't intend to go inside—just to look.

He twisted Thursday's leash around his hand, forcing her to walk close to his leg, her tail down and her back fur bristling.

Blurred reflections of himself and Thursday shone in the metal sides, as they had in Maag's helmet. The structure of Pod 56-H was so smooth that except where a different material was used for windows and the door, it appeared to be made of one single piece of metal.

A vibration Erik could feel in his chest came from the pod. He stood in front of the open door, feeling the pulsing, wondering if he dared put his head inside to get a better look.

"Trust Broadcast. Please acknowledge."

Erik wiped his hand across his eyes, sucking in his breath. The unmistakable radio voice of Trust Control was coming from inside the Helgatite pod—from the Helgatites' radio!

"Willow Sentinel acknowledges."

"Green Sentinel acknowledges."

"Triumph Sentinel acknowledges."

"Bay Sentinel acknowledges."

"Copper Sentinel acknowledges."

Erik froze. It was the Lone Sentinel's turn to acknowledge, and he wasn't by his radio. The interference had ended, and Erik wasn't standing by. But why was the Trust broadcasting at this time of day, hours past the regular Trust Broadcast time?

"Lone Sentinel acknowledges."

It was Erik's voice, but it wasn't Erik speaking. Thursday whined, tipping her head uncertainly from the pod to Erik.

"This is the Code Q check. Please report."

The radio went silent as each sentinel responded on its own channel.

The Code Q check! During the Code Q check, the sentinels were required to respond to the Trust's signal every hour. Erik was familiar with the Code Q check from the Trust Operations Manual. It was only used during an emergency when the Trust wanted the caremen to stand by their radios.

"Lone Sentinel here. Nothing to report," came Erik's own voice again from inside the pod.

Why would the Helgatites be mimicking Erik's voice to Trust Control? And if the Helgatites' radio was working, shouldn't Erik's be working, too?

Maag descended from the biosote fields toward Erik and Thursday. Erik couldn't ask Maag why his own voice was coming from inside the pod, not only because it was against protocol to ask, but also because Erik was afraid.

He stepped away from the pod, meeting the tall, silvery Maag as he approached.

"I hope I have not intruded, Maag," Erik said, struggling to keep his face smooth. "I was admiring the pod. I have never seen anything so sleekly designed." Erik felt his lips quiver and pulled them together between his teeth.

After what seemed a long time, Maag said, "It *is* a fine design, for its time. The newer pods run more efficiently and make less use of the reflective materials. Perhaps you will see one when we come to harvest the biosote."

"It would be an honor," Erik said solemnly.

"I go in to replenish now, Careman Erik."

Maag stepped inside Pod 56-H, and the door closed securely behind him.

12
THE
NEWSPAPERS

Erik's legs felt wooden, but he tried to walk casually from the pod to his house, keeping Thursday on a tight leash. His eyes were on the safety of his metal house, and he stumbled once over a tuft of grass. The Helgatites were communicating with Trust Control using Erik's voice.

But why?

A few heavy raindrops landed on his shoulders as he reached the door. Inside, newspapers were scattered around the living room, lying open and rumpled and mixed together, as if they'd been hastily skimmed and then discarded. Augusta sat in the middle of the newspapers, a pile of plastic wrappers beside her. She held out one paper in her bandaged hand.

"I found the article," she said to Erik. "Read it, and you'll see why I had to go through all your papers." She stood and offered the paper to Erik. "Here. See for yourself."

Erik waved her away. The order of the newspapers suddenly seemed foolishly unimportant. "Not right now," he said. "I have to check the radio."

"It won't work."

Erik walked past her to the radio in the corner of the living room. It must work. If the Helgatites' radio was working, then his must be, too.

"Trust Control. Please acknowledge. This is Lone Sentinel."

He heard only the hiss of static. Erik tried again, but there was still no answer.

"I told you it wouldn't work. Now will you read this?"

There was still the auxiliary radio. The supply room door stood open; the cooling motor was running, trying to cool the supplies. Erik uncovered the auxiliary radio and tried to raise Trust Control, but it, too, was silent.

"Erik," Augusta said from behind him. "I'm sorry that I messed up your newspapers, but it's important that you read this. It's about the biosote."

"The biosote?" Erik echoed.

"Yes," Augusta said, showing him the folded newspaper and tapping her finger against a small article near the bottom of the page.

Erik took the paper and read the headline aloud, " 'Biosote Diseased?' "

New Province scientists are studying two fields of biosote that appear to have been destroyed by unknown causes. The fields, in remote areas not tended by any of the caremen in the sentinel system, are small, wild fields not utilized by the Helgatites. However, scientists are studying the fields to be sure the symptoms do not spread.

"The biosote has the appearance of being burned," said Joseph Winsett of the New Province Scientific Institute.

The blackened fields were reported two weeks ago by a hiker. Scientists have discounted the theory that the biosote was killed by an electrical storm.

"Whatever it was, these fields are definitely dead," said Winsett.

"These fields are definitely dead," Erik repeated the last sentence aloud.

"I saw you go up to the biosote fields," Augusta said. "Are they dead, too? Do they look burned?"

Erik nodded.

"That's what I thought," she said, sounding almost pleased.

Erik stared at the newspaper as if it might speak and explain the significance of the article.

"But what does this have to do with the biosote here?" he asked. "The biosote the newspaper's talking about was in a wild field a couple of months ago. I don't understand why you think it's so important."

Augusta sighed. "It's as plain as day. I found another article, too. I'll get it for you, and then maybe you can figure it out."

Erik leaned his head back and rubbed his forehead. He wished Augusta would just tell him what she meant, instead of turning it into a guessing game.

"Here," Augusta said, returning to the supply room with another newspaper. "This article was printed three

weeks before the article you just read about the dead
biosote."

Erik held out his hand for the newspaper. There
didn't seem to be any point in reading old New Province
news in view of what was happening on the Lone Sentinel *now*.

Temporary Helgatite Blackout
Trust Control reported two unexplained interruptions of radio transmissions between the
Helgatite satellite station orbiting Azure and Trust
Control yesterday. Each blackout lasted more
than an hour and originated from the satellite.
Transmissions were functioning normally at press
time, and no further transmission problems were
anticipated.

"Now do you understand?" Augusta asked when
Erik put down the newspaper.

"If there's a connection, I can't see it," Erik
told her.

Augusta raised her hands in exasperation, rolling
her eyes upward. "The blackouts were part of their plan
so they could get past the Helgatite satellite and destroy
the wild biosote. Just the way your radio blacked out
when they landed here." She picked up the newspaper
and waved it. "This was when they tested their solution
to see if it would really kill the biosote. I didn't trust
them from the second Maag refused to fix Willa. They're
only here to destroy the biosote."

"But that doesn't make sense," Erik said. "If the
Helgatites destroy the biosote, they'll die. That's why

they set up the sentinel system and Trust Control, to protect the biosote. They'd be committing suicide."

Augusta looked at Erik scornfully. "Don't be stupid."

"What do you mean?"

"They aren't the real Helgatites. They're just pretending to be. If you were planning to destroy the biosote, what better place to start than on the most remote sentinel in the system? Lucky for them it's manned by one dumb kid who's never set foot off his compound."

"But they look like Helgatites. They look the way I remember them, and just like in pictures. If they're not real, who are they?"

Augusta shrugged. "I don't know. Enemies of the Helgatites, obviously."

"My father would have known if they were impostors," Erik mused aloud. "None of this would be happening if he were still alive."

Augusta stepped closer to Erik and touched his arm briefly. "Uncle Wayne's notes didn't say how your father died."

"He fell from the sentinel during an ice storm."

"I'm sorry. It must have been horrible for you."

Erik looked away from her sympathetic eyes, trying not to see again his father falling through the darkness toward the ground.

"I couldn't leave the Lone Sentinel and go to New Province. This is my home. I felt I was making the best choice by not informing Trust Control he was dead."

"And I felt I was making the best choice by leaving New Province with Willa," Augusta said quietly. "But you seem to think my decision was wrong and yours was right."

"I didn't say that."

Augusta grunted and sat on the remaining stack of newspapers. "The question is," she said, "what are we going to do about the intruders?"

Erik sat down on a box of soup. He'd learned every mechanical part of the beam, what every change in the weather might mean to the sentinel, how to live a life that kept the aloneness at bay and made him fit for the rigors of a careman. But nowhere had he learned what to do when he met Helgatites who weren't really Helgatites, when the biosote was in danger from unknown enemies, when he had deceived Trust Control and was harboring runaways from New Province. The Trust Operations Manual didn't give him answers to these problems.

"I have to think about this first," Erik said.

"You think too much," Augusta snapped.

"And you don't think enough," Erik snapped back.

Augusta stood up. "Well, while you're thinking in here, I'll go back and sit in front of the window so I can watch these impostors kill off the rest of the biosote. It shouldn't take them much longer."

She stamped out of the supply room, slamming the door behind her.

13
THE GUARD

Erik leaned against the shelves. He couldn't stand by and watch the biosote be destroyed. But what if Augusta and the newspaper were wrong and Maag was right, that the biosote would recover and grow three times as fast?

If these intruders were actually true Helgatites, Erik would jeopardize the entire colony of New Province if he tried to stop them.

But would the true Helgatites have jammed the Lone Sentinel's radios and then duplicated Erik's voice to Trust Control? And if the Trust was broadcasting a Code Q check, they must suspect a problem at the sentinels.

Erik twisted the two newspapers together. If Maag and his helpers were fake Helgatites, it might be too late to save the Lone Sentinel's biosote fields, but there were still the fields at the other sentinels. There had to be a way to get a message to the Trust.

Erik resolutely returned to the living room. The rain had stopped. Shafts of sunlight slanted through the clouds, making the raindrops on the window glisten like sparks of rainbow. The pod sat smooth and closed, still in the shadows of the clouds.

"We have to inform Trust Control of what's happening here," Erik said.

Augusta turned away from the window. "That makes perfect sense to me, but how?"

Willa pressed her hands to her head and whispered, "They're listening. It hurts."

"Who . . . " Augusta began, her eyes wide.

"What's hurting, Willa?" Erik asked.

"Look!" Augusta cried, pointing to the pod.

The door of the pod opened, and two Helgatites exited. No, Erik thought; they weren't Helgatites. They were intruders, and one of them was Maag. They were headed for the house.

"I'll go out. Don't let Thursday loose."

Augusta nodded and gripped Thursday's collar.

Water still dripped from the eaves of the house and collected in puddles on the worn path.

Maag and the other intruder met Erik at the corner of the house, near Willa and Augusta's blue vehicle.

"Greetings," Erik said, bowing low.

"Greetings, Careman Erik," Maag said in his smooth voice, bowing just as low as Erik.

"Since the rain has diminished, we have decided to complete the spraying of the biosote fields today rather than chance it will rain again tomorrow. We will begin in just a few minutes. Please stay inside your house until we have concluded our activities."

"I am scheduled to make a sentinel check shortly before dinner," Erik said, hoping Maag didn't know the afternoon check was done only during bad weather.

Maag's helmeted head tipped up toward the beam. "That will not be necessary today, Careman Erik. The beam is functioning properly. Is your animal companion inside?"

"Yes."

"It appears that your animal can defy your strength. It could be of great harm to us, so I will leave a member of our party here to watch your door and assure that your animal stays inside while we complete the spraying."

A guard! Maag was putting a guard on his house!

"I understand," Erik said. "We will do our best to keep her restrained."

Maag moved off toward the pod. The other intruder glided to a spot opposite the door and stood, his long, loose body facing the house. Erik could see only the guard's smooth protective suit. There was no sign of a weapon, but then neither had he seen a weapon in Maag's hand when he had stopped Thursday in midair.

The guard seemed clumsier than Maag, frailer and weaker. There was a slump to his narrow shoulders. When Erik passed him and bowed, the guard didn't respond.

As soon as Erik was inside and had closed and locked the door, Augusta let go of Thursday's collar. Thursday jumped at Erik and put her paws on his shoulders, licking his face.

"No licks, no licks," Erik said, forcing a loud laugh. He rubbed her neck through her thick fur.

"What's going on?" Augusta asked.

Erik put a finger to his lips and shook his head. Then he said loudly, emphasizing each word, "The Helgatites have decided to finish spraying the solution now that the rain has quit. They were worried that Thursday might get loose and attack them when they were so far from the safety of their pod. That's all."

Augusta nodded and said just as clearly, "I won't let her out of my sight."

Erik took a pad of paper and a pencil from beside the radio and wrote, "There's a guard by the door," then handed it to Augusta.

The three watched as the remaining intruders left the pod and filed into the biosote fields, carrying their containers of solution. Erik could see that the intruders weren't replenished. They moved much slower, stopping every few steps to rest or set their containers on the ground. Only Maag seemed refreshed. He walked ahead of the others, not stopping to rest or to look at the rest of his party behind him.

"What can we do?" Augusta wrote on the pad and handed it back to Erik.

"Can your vehicle get us to New Province?" Erik wrote back.

Augusta frowned and took the pad. "Maybe, but it would be slow with all the muddy ruts in the road," she wrote. Then, "If you have a map, maybe we can find an easier way." Her shoulders sagged, and she scribbled, "They'll catch us anyway—they can fly."

"We have to try," Erik penciled.

"Willa!" Augusta said as Erik opened the specially built map drawer beneath the radio table. "Let's find a fun video to watch, and then I'll fix us something to eat. We've been so busy we forgot about lunch!"

"All right, Augusta," Willa agreed amiably and sat cross-legged on the floor in front of the player.

"Ah, here's a good one," Augusta said, taking a cartridge from the shelf and putting it in the machine.

Augusta turned up the sound of the comedy play until its rollicking music seemed to bounce from the walls of the house. Thursday jumped excitedly around Augusta.

"I've always wanted to see this one," Augusta shouted over the music, clapping her hands.

Erik found the map marked "Supplier's Route: New Province to Lone Sentinel" and unfolded it on the dining table. New Province was a blue square, and the Lone Sentinel a red circle with tiny squares inside for each building. The way between the two was brown and gold, but clearly showed thin strips of river and the shadowed hills that rose up between the plains and the Lone Sentinel. The long road was a solid black line that stretched straight across the plains and twisted through the hills.

Augusta left Willa in front of the video and joined Erik. She traced her finger along the black line of the road.

"This is the only road, isn't it?" she whispered. "Our vehicle isn't powerful enough just to take off across the country; the mud on the road was bad enough."

Erik pointed to a dotted line that snaked from the edge of the hills near the Lone Sentinel compound and rejoined the solid black line of road just before the plains.

"Chad the Supplier said he uses this route when the main road is washed out or muddy. It's higher and drier, but it's so narrow it's slower for his half-track to travel."

Augusta chewed on her pencil. "It might be easier going for our smaller vehicle—if it *is* drier. Have you ever seen it?"

Erik shook his head. "I've never left the compound," he reminded her. He leaned closer to the map. There were five squares spaced along the road between New Province and the Lone Sentinel. He touched each one with a finger.

"These are suppliers' shacks," he explained quietly. "They were built so the supplier could leave spare vehicle parts or supplies for himself."

"Are you sure? We came that route, and I don't remember seeing any buildings."

"They're camouflaged so they won't be noticed by people passing by. It could mean the supplier's life if someone tampered with his shack and destroyed his emergency supplies."

"Are there radios?"

"It'd make sense to put a radio in each shack, but I don't know. The suppliers maintain the shacks; the caremen don't have anything to do with them."

"Hmmm. How long do you think it would take us to get to this supplier's shack?" Augusta asked, tapping the nearest square on the map.

The square was situated in the hills, not far from the start of the plains and shortly before the dotted trail through the hills rejoined the solid black road.

Erik measured the space with his hand. "From the map's scale and the speed you say your vehicle travels, at least an hour, maybe more, depending on the shape of the road."

"It feels useless to try, doesn't it? They'd be on us in no time with their airship." Augusta put her elbows on the table and her chin in her hands. She frowned down at the map. "Who knows what they'd do if they caught us. Probably crisp us with that growth solution of theirs."

"If there *are* radios in the shack, they might not work either," Erik said dejectedly, "just like ours."

They stared glumly at the map, with the silly comedy music surrounding them. Then looking up at the same time, they caught each other's eyes. A slow smile spread across Augusta's face, a grimly determined smile. She nodded her head at Erik. Erik nodded back.

He picked up the pad of paper again. It was too dangerous even to whisper his idea. "Maybe we can damage the pod enough to slow them down—and give us a chance."

Augusta pulled the pad toward her. "Do you have a plan?" she wrote.

Erik wasn't sure he did, but he carefully printed, "I think so."

Augusta read what he'd written and squeezed his arm with both her hands, nodding and smiling.

Erik took the pad of paper to his Reclina-Chair and began to map out his plan, while Augusta went through the cupboards looking for something to fix for lunch. He barely glanced at the slow-moving intruders in the biosote fields as he wrote.

The video blared; he and Willa and Augusta ate sandwiches, but Erik paid little attention to any of it.

The clearer his plan became, the more sorrowful he grew. Not only would it mean abandoning the Lone Sentinel for the first time in his life, it would also mean leaving Thursday behind with the intruders.

ESCAPE

"Are you ready?" Erik wrote on the pad of paper. "Do you know what to do?"

Augusta nodded, putting crackers and protein bars into the pockets of her jacket and Willa's.

"Will Willa be all right?" he wrote.

Augusta took the pad from him and wrote in her straight handwriting, "You don't have to worry about Willa when she's with me."

"All right then," Erik said, looking out the window. "It's time."

The intruders were at the upper end of the biosote fields, as far from the house as they were likely to get. Behind the intruders, nearly a third of the biosote fields now lay blackened and desolate. But the workers rested more often than they sprayed. Their movements were sluggish and erratic. Good, Erik thought; the more tired they were, the better.

"Come here, Thursday," Erik called softly.

Erik knelt on the floor, and the big dog put her head on Erik's shoulder.

"You're a good dog, Thursday, a good dog." There was more he wanted to say, but he couldn't. Thursday was his companion, his friend, more than just a pet. And he might never see her again.

He snapped the leash to her collar and handed the looped end to Augusta. Thursday wagged her tail uncertainly.

"Take care," Erik whispered. "If something goes wrong, come into the house and lock the door."

"It's going to work," Augusta whispered. "I know it will."

"Willa," she said loudly. "Thursday needs to go outside. Will you come with us?"

Willa eagerly got up from the floor.

"Put on your jacket. It's chilly outside."

Erik watched as the two girls put on their identical jackets, blending once more into their mysterious twinness. He could easily tell them apart now by the way they moved and held themselves, even when he couldn't see their faces. Was it really only a few nights ago that they'd appeared at the door of his house?

In his own pocket, Erik carried the gun his father had taught him to shoot at the borers.

At the door, Willa turned around and asked, "Aren't you coming with us, Erik?"

"I have some work I need to do here."

Augusta opened the door, and the two girls stepped out of the little house with Thursday between them.

"You must stay inside," the guard warned. His voice was the same timbre as Maag's, only flat, without Maag's musical inflections. "It is dangerous for you to come outside; the solution may be harmful to your species."

"I'm sorry," Augusta said imperiously, taking another step forward and pulling Thursday and Willa along with her. "We must come outside. Thursday, our companion animal, needs to relieve herself, and it is impossible for her to do it inside the house. We'll only be out here a short time."

As they'd planned, Augusta left the door standing open. Erik pressed himself against the wall so he could see and hear what was happening through the crack.

"But the solution may be harmful to your species," the guard repeated. "It may be dangerous. You must stay inside."

"We won't be outside long enough for it to bother us," Augusta said haughtily. Thursday growled at the guard, and Augusta tugged sharply on her leash.

"If you don't like it, why don't you come with us and make sure we come right back?" she challenged.

Without waiting for the intruder guard to answer, Augusta led Willa and Thursday away from the house, her bandaged hand through Willa's arm.

"Command your animal to relieve itself here," the guard said, pointing to the ground.

"Don't be ridiculous," Augusta told him and kept walking.

The guard lifted a suited hand toward Augusta's back. Erik touched the gun in his pocket, but the guard dropped his hand and followed, towering behind Augusta, Willa, and Thursday.

When they were fifty feet away, Erik slipped from behind the door and around the side of the house, crouching between Augusta's vehicle and the wall.

By leaning forward, Erik could see the guard following the twins and Thursday. Higher up in the biosote, the intruders rested, huddled together in a patch of sunlight, their containers of solution glistening on the ground.

Erik put his hand on the cold metal of Augusta's blue vehicle. There was no way to tell if the intruders had tampered with it. If they had and it didn't run, their plan wouldn't work.

Augusta led the guard at an angle, away from both the buildings and the biosote fields, through the new grasses and wildflowers, with Thursday sniffing the ground and pulling on her leash. Good dog.

Erik held the gun close to his chest. Staying low, he approached the pod, crawling along beside it toward the door. The wet ground soaked through the knees of his pants and made sucking sounds as he crawled. He was careful not to touch the metal sides in case Maag had turned on the field of energy.

The door of the pod was partially open as it had been when he'd heard his own voice. Crouching, he watched Augusta for the signal, holding the gun ready in his hands, going over again what they were going to do.

He was either making a good decision as a careman, or the most terrible mistake of his life.

"I wish you were here, Dad," he whispered.

Augusta raised her hand and pointed to the top of Green Grass Ridge. It was the signal.

Willa and the guard looked in the direction Augusta was pointing. Augusta leaned down and spoke to Thursday, releasing her from her leash at the same time.

Erik held his breath, unable to look away. Everything depended on this moment.

Thursday charged toward the group of intruders in the biosote field. Like her first attack on Maag, she ran low to the ground, her hackles raised and her powerful muscles speeding her across the hillside. Her long teeth gleamed between her curled lips.

Hand in hand, Augusta and Willa raced back toward the house. The guard stood, swaying like a stalk of grass, his silver-helmeted head turning from Thursday to Willa and Augusta.

Erik didn't wait to see more. He stood and fired the gun through the pod's door, careful not to touch the skin of the pod itself. He shot inside in every direction, hearing the *ping!* as the pellets hit, then a popping sound and the acrid smell of burning chemicals. He emptied all twelve pellets into the pod as fast as he could pull the release.

Willa and Augusta were nearly to the compound. Augusta was in the lead, her jacket flapping open as she ran, pulling Willa by the hand.

Erik threw down his empty gun and ran to Augusta's vehicle. He jumped into the driver's seat. Everything seemed to move foolishly slow. He didn't dare take time to look toward the biosote field. Thursday. Where was Thursday?

The little street vehicle's engine started with a whining shriek. It was easy, Augusta had said. There was nothing to driving; any fool could do it.

The vehicle lurched forward, narrowly missing the leg of the sentinel before he got it under control. He let up on the pedal and steered jerkily toward Willa and Augusta. Through the curved windshield he saw Willa stumble as Augusta forced her to run faster.

Erik stamped on the brake, and the vehicle slammed to a stop too soon, stalling.

"Let me drive!" Augusta shouted, running toward him. "Get into the other side!"

Erik threw open the driver's door for her and slid across the seat. Augusta pushed Willa roughly inside and threw herself in, starting the vehicle moving before her door was closed. Its narrow tires spun and caught on the wet ground, lurching and shuddering as Augusta pushed the pedal to the floor. Willa smiled at Erik and put her hand in his, as relaxed as if they were back in his house.

"What are they doing?" Augusta shouted over the straining engine. "Can you see them?"

Erik looked through the rear window at the jerking, bobbing scenery behind them. His stomach careened with the vehicle. The intruders in their silvery suits were leaving the biosote fields, moving in a close knot with one figure in the front: Maag.

"They're heading for the pod," he told her.

"Did you damage it?"

"Some. I don't know how much it will slow them down; I couldn't see what I was hitting." He looked at the figures again. "I don't see Thursday," he said softly.

"Thursday is sleeping," Willa said, squeezing his hand.

Augusta hunched over the steering wheel, squinting through the windshield at the smooth dirt road and the approaching hills.

"There should be a pole marking the trail that leads away from the road," Erik said, remembering the note on the map. He'd never seen it, never seen any of the scenery racing past them; it was all disorientingly strange.

"There!" Erik said, pointing. Ahead of them beside the road, a pole with peeling white paint leaned toward the hills.

"I see it." Augusta turned the wheel sharply. Willa was thrown against Erik as the car spun its tires and slewed onto the rougher trail.

There was no sign of the Lone Sentinel compound behind them now. He had truly abandoned his responsibility. When they topped a small rise, he looked again, longing for the familiar contours of Green Grass Ridge and the spidery tower that held the beam. He saw only the surrounding hills of brown. Yet the beam sliced past above them like a distant flash of lightning, the normalcy of its rotation a brief reassurance.

The vehicle jumped and lurched, spinning its street tires and throwing up mud as Augusta pushed it to its limits. She wrenched the wheel from side to side as she tried to avoid the ruts and rocks in their path.

"I wish this thing wasn't so slow," Augusta muttered.

The scenery flashed past Erik's eyes. Surely if they went any faster, they'd be flying! He pulled the map from his pocket and unfolded it on his lap. He could barely read it in the bouncing vehicle.

"We should be coming to the first in a series of rocky hills on our right," Erik said.

"That must be it," Augusta said, nodding ahead.

Through the mud-spattered window, Erik saw the

slope of a steep hill. Bright white rocks of varying sizes were scattered across its face. They stood out with a brilliant deep shine, almost transparent. As the track curved around the hill, more of the strange white hills were exposed.

"Just keep following the trail," Erik told Augusta. "It winds through more hills like these, then lower hills before we come to the supplier's shack." He glanced from the map to the vehicle's odometer and calculated the miles.

"Your odometer should read about 32451 when we reach the shack."

Augusta nodded grimly. "Do you think they're following us yet?"

Behind them, all around them, the blue sky hung soft and empty.

15
THE FINAL CHANCE

Willa drowsed between Erik and Augusta, her head bumping against his shoulder and waking her whenever the vehicle jerked or bumped.

The little blue vehicle valiantly churned through the mud and whined up and down the rough trail that wove through the hills, sometimes traveling slower than a walk. Once it mired in mud, helplessly spinning its wheels and going nowhere until Erik jumped out and pushed it free.

They passed a few more hills of brilliant white rocks and then were back in the plain brown hills with their gray rocks and scattered vegetation. Erik's heart pounded at their closeness. He was used to wide spaces that let him see in every direction. These steep little hills seemed to squeeze the vehicle between them.

He continually glanced out the windows, searching for any sign of the pod, but the hills were so steep that they wouldn't be able to see it unless it was directly overhead.

A shadow passed above them, keeping pace with the vehicle, and Erik was certain it was the intruders. He was about to tell Augusta to stop—that maybe the intruders would be easier on them if they surrendered— when Willa pointed and sighed.

"Look," she said. "There's a struckie. They look like giant bugs."

A struckie. The shadow was only a struckie. It landed on the hill in front of them and watched them pass, turning its small beaked head on its long neck and holding to the hill with its four feet. Willa was right. It *was* like a giant insect.

"We don't have struckies at home," Willa said. "I like the way they look."

"They're too shy to come near New Province," Augusta explained to Erik. "What good are they anyway? The only thing they do is eat the biosote."

"Maybe they should be put in homes for useless birds," Willa said.

Augusta gasped. "Not even a struckie deserves to be locked in a home," she said fiercely.

In a small voice, Willa said, "I wish we were home again, don't you, Augusta?"

"You'd like to be back in New Province?" Augusta asked, taking her eyes off the trail.

"Mmm-hmm, in our bedroom with the red flowers on the window."

Augusta drove on, staring straight ahead, biting her lower lip.

When the odometer read 32450, Erik told Augusta, "We'd better start looking for the supplier's shack." They were still traveling through the close brown hills. "The shacks are supposed to look like their surroundings, so I guess we're looking for some kind of brown building."

"That's not a lot of help, is it?" Augusta asked, slowing the vehicle. She and Erik rolled down their windows, and as they inched along, peered at rocks, bulges, and discolorations for anything that might be a camouflaged building. Every second gave the intruders more time to catch up.

The odometer turned to 32451. The hillsides remained ordinary hillsides, with scattered rocks, tough long-rooted grasses, and occasionally a borer curiously sticking its head out of its burrow.

When the odometer turned to 32452, Augusta tapped her fingers along the steering wheel and asked, "Do you think we missed it? Should we turn around?"

"Let's try going a little farther," Erik said, leaning his head out the window. "I might have calculated the miles wrong."

"How old is that map? Maybe the shack isn't there anymore."

"If that were true, the Trust would have sent a new map."

Augusta brought the vehicle to an abrupt stop. Erik grabbed Willa so she wouldn't plunge into the window.

"What's that?" Augusta asked, pointing to the hills on her side of the vehicle.

Erik jumped out and scanned the hill before he saw it, too: a tiny building nestled into a cleft in the hill. It was constructed of the same metal as Erik's house, only this was colored a mottled brown. It was almost invisible, set back so the slope of the hill formed its roof. From above, it would just be a part of the hill.

"That has to be it," Erik said. "Let's go take a look at it."

Augusta steered the vehicle as close to the foot of the hill as possible and turned off the engine. The buzzing engine echoed between the hills for several seconds, and then the day was completely silent.

There was no path to the shack; it was as if no one had ever gone there. The door lay about sixty feet up the hill, and then the rocky slope extended beyond the shack for another thirty or forty feet.

They didn't talk as they climbed toward the windowless building. Augusta and Willa panted behind Erik as they scrambled to keep up. He knew Augusta must be thinking what he was, that this was their final chance, there wasn't time to try anything else.

The shack was no wider than Erik's spread arms and only slightly taller than the top of his head.

"Can you open it?" Augusta asked, sliding her hand across the door.

Erik turned the knob. The door didn't move. "The suppliers' shacks are supposed to be unlocked," he said. He put his shoulder to the door and shoved.

With a creak, the door opened inward. The shack smelled of having been closed up. The light through the open door showed a bank of shelves against the back wall holding boxes of food and first-aid supplies.

In the middle of the shelves, covered by clear plastic, sat a radio.

"It's a radio!" Augusta said, laughing and squeezing in beside Erik. "Your plan worked, Erik. Let's call for help and get these impostors blown off Azure!"

There was a chance. With the radio, they had a chance.

"Oh Augusta," Willa cried from the open door. "It's them." She stared toward the north with her ears covered.

Erik looked across the hills to where he knew the Lone Sentinel lay. Just rising into view, he saw the pod. It was coming toward them.

16
CODE D

"It's the pod," Erik said. "I couldn't have done much damage to it after all."

Augusta pulled Willa, her hands still over her ears, into the shack. "You gave us time to get here," she told Erik. "If we stay inside, maybe they won't find us."

Erik uncovered the radio, and Willa and Augusta squeezed together to give him more room. The radio was an older model, one with dials that had to be set and coordinated to make a call. He leaned over it and turned the dials. A low orange light came from the radio, accompanied by a hum of static.

"It works!" Augusta said.

"So far."

Augusta put her hand on the radio. "Wait," she said.

Erik straightened. "Wait? What for? We don't have time to waste."

"Could the intruders disrupt the radio once you started transmitting?"

"I don't know. Probably."

Augusta sucked in her cheeks, then said in a rush, "Can't you call the Helgatites instead of Trust Control?"

"Why? The proper order is to call Trust Control first, for directions. They can tell us what procedures to follow."

"But if the intruders interrupt your call to the Trust, you won't have gained anything. Besides, the Trust can't get here in time to help us now. If you call the Helgatites at their satellite station, maybe they can get here quicker. You *can* call them, can't you?"

Erik nodded. "A Code D call. It's a distress signal, only to be used in the most dire emergencies."

Augusta put her hands on her hips. "What do you call this, a minor emergency?"

Erik couldn't help smiling. "It probably couldn't get much more dire."

"Can't you hurry, then? They're getting closer."

Through the open door, Erik could see the pod, still a long way off, swooping and curving as it followed their tracks along the high trail that branched from the main road. The air trembled with its approach.

"Close the door, and I'll get started," Erik said, and turned back to the radio.

Except for the faint golden light from the radio that let him read its meters and dials, the interior of the shack went dark. The Code D call was an automatic emergency signal intended only for the Helgatite satellite orbiting Azure. It transmitted on a frequency never used on the planet Azure itself, a frequency specific to the Helgatites. If he were to turn it on, would he be calling the intruders right to their hiding place?

Yet Augusta was right: if he called Trust Control, he risked losing the transmission before he even informed them of the situation. And he might get through with a Code D call. Besides, as she said, Trust Control couldn't help. They were on their own.

Erik carefully set the dials to transmit the D call. The radio whined, shriller and shriller, until it faded away at its highest register. The meter pulsed regularly, indicating that the call was going out. But to whom?

Erik sat on the floor opposite Willa and Augusta in the dark, cool shack. This must be what it felt like to be a borer, he thought, always in the darkness and uncertain of what was going on above you.

"It's not as if the Helgatites are just around the corner, is it?" Augusta asked. "They're not going to be dropping by in the next five minutes to check on our problems."

"If there's a ship at the satellite station, it wouldn't take them all that long to reach us."

"How long?"

"I don't know," Erik admitted. The radio gave off such a faint light that Erik could barely make out Augusta's and Willa's features. Without their usual differences in expression, they formed completely identical shadows.

"What do you think the intruders will do if they find us?" Augusta asked.

Erik didn't answer. He didn't want even to consider that possibility. He strained to hear if the pod were any closer, but no sound penetrated the shack.

"Are you sorry you didn't tell the Trust that your father was dead?" Augusta whispered.

Erik thought. If he'd reported his father's death, they wouldn't be in the danger they were facing right now.

"No," he told Augusta. "I couldn't have left the Lone Sentinel to live with strangers, not with all those people. This is better. This is my home."

"It *is* very beautiful, in a desolate sort of way. I feel as if I can breathe here, as if there's room to be myself. . . . Oh, I can't explain it."

Erik knew exactly what she meant. "Are you sorry you left New Province the way you did?" he asked.

Now Augusta paused. "I'll give you a better answer when we find out how all this ends." She laughed drily. "I think I made the best decision . . . for both Willa and me. No matter what happens, at least she's with me. We're each other's only family."

Erik reached out in the small space and touched her arm. She put her hand in his, and they sat that way without saying any more.

The stock on the shelves began to rattle. The door shook. Augusta squeezed Erik's hand tighter. Willa covered her ears and laid her head on Augusta's shoulder.

"They must be crisscrossing the hills looking for us," Erik whispered. "At least we know the Code D signal isn't calling them directly to us."

Augusta jerked her hand free and leaned toward him, pushing her face next to his. "The vehicle!" she hissed. "We left it in plain sight at the bottom of the hill."

Erik couldn't believe he'd forgotten the unnaturally blue vehicle. The intruders had to see it eventually. And if they set the pod down there, it wouldn't take Maag long to find the shack. Not Maag. How could Erik have been so stupid?

The radio screeched, and the meters dropped, losing the Code D frequency. Erik jumped up and crouched in front of the radio. The pod's vibrations had shaken the radio's fine tuning.

Erik concentrated on giving the dials the minutest touches with his fingertips to bring the meters back into alignment. He almost had it when he stopped, deliberately wrenching the dials off alignment. There was no sense in continuing to broadcast the D call. Either the Helgatite satellite had received it by now, or they'd never receive it. The radio glowed, tuned to no frequency, only giving them light.

"I turned off the D call," he said. "We shouldn't . . . " He squinted into the shadows. Only Willa sat there, her eyes closed and her hands clasped on her lap.

"Where's Augusta?" Erik demanded.

Willa opened her eyes and said dreamily, "Augusta took Uncle Wayne's vehicle so the intruders could see it."

Erik threw open the door of the supplier's shack. He heard the buzzing of the vehicle's engine, and worse, above him he heard the hum of the intruders' pod.

Augusta was leading the intruders away from the supplier's shack, away from Erik and Willa, and toward the open plains.

"Augusta!" Erik shouted, knowing it was impossible for her to hear him. And even if she could hear him, he knew she wouldn't stop.

17
ONTO THE PLAINS

The pod flew low, skimming the hilltops, following Augusta as she drove around and between the hills. Erik couldn't see the vehicle, only hear its engine now and then. He knew her path because of the way the pod flew in the air above her.

If Augusta stayed in the relative protection of the hills, he thought, she might have a chance. The hills crowded so close together that the intruders might not be able to—Erik shuddered—they might not be able to get a clear shot at her.

"Willa," Erik said. "I'm going to climb to the top of this hill. You wait here until I get back."

"I can't. Augusta told me not to leave you, not for anything," she said, with such complete certainty Erik knew it was pointless to argue.

So he and Willa both climbed the rise above the supplier's shack and lay on the narrow crest of the hill.

Not far to the south, the hills sloped down, leveling into the grassy plains.

The pod flew away from Erik and Willa, then turned a little, toward the south. Suddenly, the vehicle burst out of the hills. The bright blue was clearly visible. Bouncing and jerking, it threw up mud behind its little wheels as it sped straight out into the plains.

"Oh no. Why'd she do that?" Erik asked aloud.

There was no more protection for Augusta, only the open prairie with its spring vegetation, not a single tree. The pod leisurely closed in. It floated along behind Augusta, swaying and bobbing gently in the air.

Erik clenched his fists. He could do nothing. It was like watching his father fall all over again.

The pod was directly above Augusta. The little blue vehicle paused in its dash and began a grotesque dance. It turned end over end. Then it rolled sideways. Again and again. As it rolled, its metal body became battered and misshapen, flattening into itself.

"No!" Willa screamed, and yanked her hand from Erik's. Gasping, she rose and started down the hill, scrambling and sliding, toward the plains and Augusta. Erik jumped up and threw himself at her. He caught her around the legs, knocking her to the ground.

"Augusta!" she cried, kicking and hitting at Erik, trying to get away. "It's Augusta! She's hurt! Let me go!"

Erik held on tighter. "It's too dangerous, Willa. We'll go to Augusta, I promise. As soon as the intruders leave, we'll go to her."

As he repeated his words, Willa gradually quit fighting, until she lay on the ground sobbing, mud streaking her face and clothes.

The pod circled the vehicle where it lay upside down with its wheels still turning. There was no movement near the vehicle. The pod circled, two, three times. Erik thought it was about to land, but instead it hovered near the overturned vehicle, then rose higher into the air.

"Willa. We have to get back inside now. Then we'll go to Augusta."

The pod moved out over the plains. It turned in a wide circle and headed back toward the hills. Erik pulled Willa by the wrist back down the hill. The rocks rolled beneath their feet as they raced for the door of the shack.

He closed the door behind them, and he and Willa dropped to the rough floor.

Erik put his finger to his lips but Willa didn't move, she simply sat with her eyes closed. The pod's vibrations grew louder, then more distant. The intruders were searching the hills, suspecting that all three of them hadn't been in the vehicle. Erik held his breath as the pod came closer again, then moved off once more.

Finally the vibrations ended. But still Erik waited in the dark shack with Willa.

Willa raised her head. Her voice faltered. "The intruders are gone, Erik. Can we go to Augusta now?"

He didn't doubt her. "Yes, we'll go now."

Willa lifted her hand, and Erik helped her up. Her fingers were icy cold.

They followed the vehicle's tracks toward the open plain. Erik tried to make Willa walk beside him, but she ran ahead until she was worn out and red-faced, then walked as fast as she could until she was rested enough to run again.

The hills were silent in the late afternoon sun. Here and there hardy spring flowers clung to the sunny slopes. Erik tried not to think of Augusta.

Once Willa looked up at him and said in a tight voice, "I don't feel her, Erik."

As they left the hills and entered the wide open plain, Erik scanned the sky, afraid the pod might come racing back to find them.

Willa ran ahead of him again, holding her side. Now the tracks in front of them changed. The tire prints disappeared, and a few yards ahead there was a torn gash in the earth where the vehicle had landed during its somersaulting roll. Water seeped into the ruts made by its flipping.

It seemed pitifully small when they found it. It lay battered and scarred. The windows were broken outward, and the roof was crushed.

"Wait, Willa," Erik said, pulling her back from the vehicle. The passenger door was open. Mud and grass were stuck to the seat. Erik bent down and looked through the broken windshield.

Augusta wasn't inside.

"She's not here, Willa. She might have jumped out."

Willa didn't seem to hear or understand. She stood silently on the other side of the vehicle, her eyes vacant.

"I'm going to look for Augusta," Erik told her, but Willa didn't respond.

The new prairie grass was already to Erik's knees. By the end of the short summer, its stalks would turn to brown and stand as tall as his waist. He began his search for Augusta by trudging in circles around the wrecked vehicle, probing into the grass for her slight form.

He almost missed her. His eye was caught by the white bandage that still wrapped her outflung hand. She was only a small mark in the deep prairie grasses.

Augusta lay on her back with her legs folded beneath her. Blood was matted into her hair and across her ear. Her face was pale and still.

"Augusta."

She didn't move. Erik knelt beside her and took the wrist of her bandaged hand. At first he felt nothing. He took off his outer shirt and put it over her and felt for a pulse again. It was faint: an unsteady flutter.

"Augusta, you're going to be fine. Willa and I are here to take care of you. You did a stupid thing—a stupid, brave thing."

Erik kept his fingers on the barely perceptible pulse. He was afraid that if he let go, it might slip away. He turned and looked back at Willa. She stood exactly as he'd left her.

"Willa," he called. "I found Augusta."

A breeze came up from the plain and fluffed Willa's dark hair across her face. She made no move to brush it out of her eyes.

Erik looked from Willa to Augusta. He had no medical supplies, and he was afraid to move Augusta. Where would he move her to, anyway? And something seemed to be wrong with Willa. How could he possibly take care of both of them at once?

"Willa," he tried again. "Come here and help me with Augusta."

Willa stood unmoving, facing the open plain, a small dark statue in the waving grass.

Was Augusta's pulse even more feeble? Erik rubbed her arm and covered her more closely with his shirt. The breeze blew stronger, whipping off the plain into his face.

He raised his head, and that was when he saw it.

It was silent, without vibration. So silent it hadn't produced a tremor of awareness or suspicion. A silvery air vehicle, skimming low across the plain, coming straight at them.

Erik searched wildly. There was no shelter, no place to hide. Just the prairie grasses and the bright blue vehicle that marked their presence.

18
ANSWERS

The prairie grasses flattened to pale waves in the wake of the airship. There was no use trying to hide. Erik knelt beside Augusta and watched the advancing ship. It was smaller than Pod 56-H. Its shape was different, too—sleeker, more elongated. Its nose came to a rounded point, and a single fin rose from its back. It appeared lighter and faster than the other pod, more maneuverable. There was a sense of darting in its oncoming movement.

Willa didn't move or seem to notice the danger they were facing. Augusta lay as still as when he'd found her. Blood seeped from the cut in her head.

The airship flew straight toward them, never wavering in its approach. It came silently, more frightening than the heart-pounding vibrations of Pod 56-H. His only hope was that the ship was coming onward so swiftly that it might pass over them and continue into the hills.

But the ship abruptly stopped less than thirty feet away, hovering three feet above the ground as if it were considering the three figures. A wash of warm air blew against Erik and pressed his clothes tight against his body.

The airship held itself afloat so quietly that Erik heard the breezes passing through the grass. Like an enlarging circle, a door opened near the underside of the ship. A ramp descended silently to the ground. There were no stabilizers to hold the air vehicle level or in its place; it simply hovered. Steady and still.

Erik wished for at least the puny reassurance of the pellet gun. He stood, his back straight, remembering how he'd stood when the intruders had first landed. He wouldn't let them see his fear.

A figure descended the ramp. First its feet in heavily soled boots, continuing on up the legs in the same material. It was the same silvery fabric as Maag's. A helmeted head rose from a body with the narrowest of shoulders. At the bottom of the ramp, the figure turned its entire body and faced Erik. A second figure descended the ramp and stood to the right of the first. It was identical, except smaller.

"You have been damaged," the first figure said in a high melodic voice.

Erik searched the smooth, smoky shield of the helmet. He couldn't make out any features, just as he hadn't been able to see through Maag's helmet.

Erik nodded toward Augusta on the ground. "My guest was in the vehicle when it was wrecked." He waved a hand toward Willa. "She . . . something's wrong with her, too."

"Are you responsible for the D call?" the first alien asked.

Erik studied the figures carefully. They stood with the same self-assurance as Maag. But would the intruders know about the Code D call?

"I transmitted the D call," Erik admitted. "Only me, Careman Erik of the Lone Sentinel. My companions are only visiting me. They had no part in it."

The two figures stood side by side, observing Erik. "Why did you call us?" the first alien asked. He raised a gloved hand to take in Augusta, Willa, and the damaged vehicle. "Is this your emergency?"

"No . . . I mean yes, it *is* an emergency. But this isn't why we transmitted the Code D." Erik stopped and caught his breath. "There are intruders at the Lone Sentinel. They say they're Helgatites. They've been spraying the biosote fields with a solution they claim will make the biosote grow faster."

"We know of no such solution," the second figure said in the same high voice, like singing. "*We* are the Helgatites."

It was true, then. He'd practically invited the intruders to destroy the biosote.

"I think the solution kills the biosote. Maag said . . . "

"Maag?" the two Helgatites voiced at once. The second Helgatite asked, "Maag is here?"

"Yes. With a crew of eight." Erik briefly explained what the intruders and Pod 56-H looked like.

The Helgatites leaned toward each other. They said nothing in words, but Erik was sure they were communicating with each other.

"You were right to use the Code D call, Careman,"

the first Helgatite said. "We've had warnings of possible trouble, and have had intermittent radio problems in the past two days."

"I have failed in my duty as a careman by not recognizing the impostors for what they are," Erik said, bowing his head.

"Maag *is* a Helgatite, although his crew is not. Until recently, Maag was a Helgatite of power. He committed crimes against our society and was stripped of his powers. Before he disappeared a number of months ago, he swore vengeance on all Helgatites. He escaped to a nearby planet similar to ours, populated by the Duveans."

"I'm going to consult with our major ship," the smaller Helgatite said, and ascended the ramp, its body loose and flowing.

"My radio has been out. They're transmitting a recording of my voice," Erik told the Helgatite. "Could they be doing the same thing at the other sentinels?"

"We can't be sure until we inspect the sentinels. We'll send other transports to investigate. We didn't know what to expect when we received your D call. We approached from across the plain to avoid the beam."

"The beam?" Erik asked. All his questions were against the protocol laid out in the manual. But what did protocol matter now? "The Lone Sentinel's beam? Why?"

"It has been activated."

Activated. That was one of the settings Erik knew how to program, but only the Trust and the Helgatites understood what it did.

"When the beam is activated," the Helgatite explained, "it destroys any object in its path."

The smaller Helgatite returned from the transport, and once again the two Helgatites communicated without words.

"Our planet is under attack by the Duveans," the first Helgatite explained calmly to Erik. "The main battle is taking place in the vicinity of our general supply of biosote."

"But why the Duveans?" Erik asked.

"The Duveans are a greedy race. Maag organized them in this attempt at revenge. The crew here with Maag is probably Duvean, and Pod 56-H, as you call it, is certainly an inferior Duvean airship."

"Do you have to return to your planet to fight the Duveans?"

"Our duty is here on Azure first," said the smaller Helgatite. He pointed to Willa and Augusta. "Should we look to your companions now?"

"Please," Erik said hopefully. He recalled the stories of the Helgatites' healing powers. "They are Willa and Augusta, my guests. Augusta was hurt when she drew Maag and the Duveans away from the shack where I was transmitting the Code D call."

Erik stood aside, and the two Helgatites moved close to Augusta. They leaned their thin bodies over her, looking for long moments without touching her.

Augusta's face was like the clear white stones he'd seen in the first hills after they left the Lone Sentinel, as if she were turning transparent.

The Helgatites went to Willa, who still looked stonily out at the plain. The Helgatites were silent in their observations, avoiding any touch with either girl.

Finally they faced Erik from the other side of Augusta. "It will be a decision of your making, Careman Erik," said the first Helgatite.

Erik nodded.

"If we are to help your guests, we must take them to our major ship, but you would have to stay behind. Our transport could not carry all three of you. If we do this, time in dealing with Maag will be lost. We would ask you to risk greater danger, until we can return to deal with the Duveans."

"Or," said the second Helgatite, "we can deal with Maag and the Duveans now and tend to your guests afterward . . . "

" . . . which would risk their lives," Erik finished.

"That is correct. Augusta is gravely injured."

"Could Maag and the Duveans destroy the Lone Sentinel?" Erik asked.

"They do have that capability."

Erik looked down at Augusta lying so still under his shirt. He didn't think Willa had even blinked her eyes.

"Tell me what I should do while you take Willa and Augusta to your major ship," Erik said.

"That is a wise decision, Careman," said the first Helgatite. "First, we ask that you put your guests into our transport. You must avoid entering the transport yourself. Your combined weights would be destructive."

"But if I lift Augusta," Erik said uncertainly, "her injuries . . . "

"Move her as little as possible," said the Helgatite.

"We cannot lift her in your atmosphere."

Erik slipped his hands beneath Augusta. Trying to keep her level and to support her as much as he could, he lifted her into his arms. She made no movement, no sound.

"Stand inside the transport's opening, but avoid stepping on the ramp," the Helgatites directed. "Lay Augusta on the floor to the left and Willa to the right."

Erik did as he was told. When he bent under the hovering transport, he braced himself to feel heat from the ship or the force field that kept the transport suspended. But there was no sense of power or mechanism, only the curiously floating airship.

He stood up inside the ship's round opening. Its smooth floor was level with his waist and seemed to give as he laid Augusta down. He left his shirt covering her and smoothed her hair carefully away from the cut in her head. He squeezed her hand once and tucked it under the shirt.

Erik turned to go for Willa, but she already stood behind him, her eyes vacant and her body stiff.

"Willa," he said, but she made no sign of having heard him. "I'm going to lift you into the transport, Willa, so you can be with Augusta. The Helgatites will take care of you both."

Willa went limp as he laid her down on the floor opposite Augusta. The smooth, oddly buoyant interior of the transport glowed from an unseen light.

"Goodbye, Willa," he said softly, and stepped out from under the transport.

The two Helgatites stood close together waiting for him.

"They're ready," Erik said. "What is it I have to do?"

"You must turn off the beam," the taller Helgatite said, "even if you have to destroy the Lone Sentinel to do it."

19
GOING BACK

The Helgatite transport carrying Augusta and Willa and the two Helgatites silently reversed itself and skimmed back across the plain the way it had come. The soundless engines propelled it away so swiftly that the grasses in front of Erik were still flattened when the transport disappeared from view.

The wind came up stronger off the plain, sighing through the grasses in low whispers and hisses. The plains stretched away in front of him, the long grasses rippling and swirling in currents. Above him, a struckie stretched its wings on the wind and called in a monotone whistle. It was a lonely place.

Erik turned away from the prairie and hiked toward the hills, back toward the Lone Sentinel. He set his pace in long deliberate strides, matching his breathing to his steps. He didn't want to be overtired when he reached the Lone Sentinel. He needed to be fresh to do what the Helgatites asked.

To turn off the beam, even if he had to destroy the Lone Sentinel.

If Maag and the Duveans discovered he was still alive, they would try to destroy him. But if the intruders believed he and the girls were dead, they might take more time to kill the biosote. They might stop and rest. Some of the biosote could still be saved.

The winds swept mournfully between the hills, greeting Erik full in the face as he rounded each one. The closed-in feeling pressed on him again. The hills were more crowded than he remembered, as if they'd shouldered closer together after he and Willa and Augusta had passed through in the vehicle.

When he was sure of his bearings, Erik left the trail and cut across the tops of the hills, dropping down again into the hills of white rocks. Their clear whiteness surrounded him. Even the air felt white.

Without breaking stride, he picked up one of the white rocks and slipped it into his pants pocket. It bumped against his leg with each step. Its weight was reassuring, like an anchor.

Finally he arrived on the crest of the final hill before the Lone Sentinel. He dropped to his stomach and peered down at his home. It was close to evening now. The daylight would soon fade.

The beam circled through the air so fast that it looked like a canopy of light over the compound. It spun at a forty-five-degree angle. That way, Erik realized, not only did it keep any airship from landing, but it kept Maag and the Duveans trapped beneath it. Maag would have to shut down the beam himself before his pod could lift off.

But that wouldn't happen until all of the biosote was destroyed.

He counted only four of the silver-suited Duveans in the biosote field. Two of them stood unmoving beside their containers of solution, their helmeted heads bent.

Where were the others? Inside the pod replenishing? He couldn't see any guards by the house or the pod. Erik scanned the buildings and grounds for Maag's distinctive presence. Could he be inside the pod replenishing, too? Maag was the greatest threat, the most dangerous to Erik's mission.

Less than half of the biosote was blackened from the solution. Yet all that was black was unusable, dead. He reminded himself that *all* of it would be dead already if he and Augusta hadn't disrupted Maag's plan. If any of the biosote could be saved, the hardest job lay ahead.

Erik jumped up and ran down the hill toward the compound. He concentrated on the ground in front of him, hurtling himself between each scant piece of protection, dodging behind a large rock, zigzagging between small bushes, leaping an open borer's hole.

He kept his eyes on his route, and suddenly he was in the shade of his house. He threw himself to the ground, panting, expecting to see a silver-suited figure standing over him, to hear melodic voices telling him he was caught.

The wind blew coolly across him. The only other sound was the accelerated passing of the beam, the hum of the mechanism at a high-pitched whir. He waited. No Duvean appeared.

Erik crept close to the wall of his house, working himself along its length with his back against the metal.

Another piece of open ground stretched between the house and the shed at the foot of the sentinel.

The shed door stood open. The lock hung from the frame, broken. In the biosote field, Erik could see that the four Duveans were at the point of exhaustion. Even the two who had been spraying had now quit.

Erik stepped away from the house and slowly walked across the open space toward the shed, eyeing the open door.

There were no other movements, no alarms, nothing to indicate that he'd been spotted.

Three more steps. Two. One. He slipped inside the shadowy shed and sat at the sentinel's controls, letting his body slump.

For a few moments, he closed his eyes and breathed steadily, counting each breath. He had to be under control when he shut down the beam.

The switch that turned off the beam couldn't be accidentally or mistakenly thrown. A series of digital controls had to be set before the switch could be pulled. If even one digit was incorrect, the series had to be started all over again. He had to get it right the first time; there might not be time to begin the entire procedure again.

Erik began the steps. He turned each dial to set the digital readout in a series of descending prime numbers.

After the last number he looked back over the lit displays to be sure there was no mistake. He whispered the series aloud.

"857. 311. 223. 127. 13."

They were all correct.

The switch that turned off the beam was on the opposite wall of the shed. All Erik had to do now was walk five steps across the room and pull it.

Rustling sounded from behind the shelves between Erik and the wall. Erik froze. Movement came again. Louder. More rustling, then a thump.

Erik turned slowly toward the sound and peered into the shadows. Had he been found out after all?

Two eyes glared at him from behind the shelf, gleaming red. A deep warning growl rumbled from the dark space.

"Thursday!"

Erik took a step toward the corner, his hand out. Thursday was alive! The red eyes peered steadily back at him, unblinking. The low growl turned more threatening. Erik stepped back.

"Thursday," he whispered. "Good girl. It's me, Erik. Come here, girl." He held out his hand, palm up, as close as he dared.

"Good Thursday," he coaxed.

The red eyes lowered in the shadows, and Erik knew that Thursday was crouching, tensing her body. She was readying herself to spring at him.

20
WAITING

Erik knelt on one knee and held his hands open in front of him.

"I didn't want to leave you, Thursday," he whispered. "It was the only way. You're a brave dog."

Thursday didn't move. Whatever Maag or the Duveans had done to her, it was Erik's fault.

"I'm sorry, Thursday."

Thursday wasn't his pet now. She was wild. Dangerous. If she attacked him, he stood as much chance as if Maag and the Duveans were to find him.

A shadow filled the shed. Erik looked up to see a tall figure in the doorway, darkened to blackness by the light behind it.

"Well, Careman Erik. I see you were fortunate to have escaped the terrible accident that befell your guests."

It was Maag. From Erik's position on his knee, Maag was gigantic, taller than the doorway. Erik was trapped.

"It was no accident," he said.

"It was unnecessary," Maag said. "If you had behaved as a proper careman and been obedient to the Trust rules, none of these unfortunate events would have taken place."

"You can stop pretending," Erik said. "I know you're a criminal."

Maag regarded him. "Your accusations will not further the relationship between the Helgatites and the people of New Province. Aren't you aware of the debt your race owes us?"

"Quit pretending," Erik demanded angrily. "I know you're an impostor. You and the Duveans are destroying the biosote."

Maag shook. His body fluttered.

"Duveans?" he said pleasantly. "Where did you learn that name? Could it have been . . . "

Everything happened at once. Thursday burst silently from behind the shelves. Her fur stood out like electricity. Her teeth were bared and her sharp fangs flashed. She lunged at Maag in a deadly rage. Erik jumped for the switch that turned off the beam. His hand slid on the lever, but his fingers caught it, and he pulled downward.

Maag raised his hand toward Thursday.

"No!" Erik screamed at Maag. This time he knew Maag would do more than simply stun Thursday. He threw himself after Thursday, straight at Maag, both arms out to knock Maag's hand out of the way.

Thursday was faster than either Erik or Maag. Her hurtling attack caught Maag before he could use the weapon built into his gloved suit.

She locked her jaws onto Maag's silver-suited arm, her teeth viciously tearing the shiny material, exposing Maag to the Azure atmosphere. Maag screamed, a bubbling high-pitched squeal that rang in Erik's ears long after it was abruptly cut off.

Erik plowed into Maag's falling figure with his shoulder. It was like charging against a hanging curtain. There was no substance to Maag, only a flattened, falling silver suit.

Thursday raged at the suited arm, furiously ripping and shaking and growling. A terrible stench filled the shed, a smell like rotting garbage. Erik coughed and rolled away from Thursday and the collapsed suit.

The silver suit lay crumpled like a piece of discarded clothing. There was no doubt that Maag was dead.

Erik backed away from Thursday while she let loose her fury against Maag and the Duveans. She savagely shook and bit at the suit, lunging at it again and again.

Through the shed window, he saw the Duveans drop their containers of solution in the biosote field and hurry across the blackened biosote toward their pod. The beam was down. The Duveans were unprotected.

Thursday dropped the limp silver suit and turned toward Erik, her teeth still bared.

"Good girl," Erik said softly, holding out his hand. "Come here, Thursday."

Erik slowly hunkered down. Thursday pawed the suit one more time and limped to Erik. He didn't move.

Thursday leaned against Erik's shoulder, and Erik hugged her, putting his face into her fur and smelling her familiar warm smell. Thursday lifted her head and licked Erik's face.

Without the hum of the mechanisms turning the Lone Sentinel's beam, the air was deadly still. Then the shed shook with the sounds of the pod's power source. Erik watched the pod take off, rising straight into the darkening sky. The Duveans weren't waiting to discover what had happened to Maag. They obviously knew that their only hope lay in getting away from Azure at once.

Descending at an angle from higher in the sky, Erik saw another craft. This one was easily five times the size of the pod. The pod veered away from the approaching ship, rising faster and higher.

The two airships rose skyward, maneuvering together, then apart. The pod could make tighter turns and dodge away from the bigger ship, but the big ship was faster. Soon Erik only caught glimpses of silver as the ships climbed and chased one another.

A flash shocked the evening sky, accompanied by a spiraling trail of thick white smoke. Erik studied it intently for a clue as to which ship had exploded, the Helgatite or the Duvean—or even both.

Except for the smoking trail, the sky was empty.

"What do you make of it, Thursday?" he asked, rubbing behind her ears.

They stood like that, watching the silent sky, until Erik realized there was nothing more to be seen. The white smoke faded to a few wisps in the sky, like thin strands of cloud.

"We may as well go inside," Erik said to Thursday. "We can only wait now."

Inside, there was no sign that the Duveans had entered his house. The chairs were still pulled in front of the window where he and Willa and Augusta had sat to watch the intruders, thinking they were about to meet the Helgatites. It had been so simple to trick him.

And Willa and Augusta. What was happening to them?

Erik sat on the floor and examined Thursday's paw. She yelped when he probed too deep, but he couldn't feel any broken bones or find any cuts.

"Sorry, girl," Erik apologized, letting go of her paw.

"Lone Sentinel, this is the Helgatite major ship. Please acknowledge."

The radio!

Erik knocked over a chair in his hurry to reach the radio. He should have tried to call Trust Control as soon as the pod left the Lone Sentinel. Another mistake.

But it was the Helgatites calling. The Helgatites were the victors of the sky battle.

"Lone Sentinel here," he responded, his voice quavering.

"We will be landing briefly, Lone Sentinel. Please be prepared to come aboard. We will depart immediately for New Province."

New Province! The Helgatites were taking him off the Lone Sentinel. He'd failed to be the careman they'd expected, and now they were removing him.

"Lone Sentinel acknowledges," he responded heavily.

21
LEAVING

Erik called Trust Control. The radio worked flawlessly.

"The Helgatites have apprised us of your situation, Lone Sentinel," said the familiar voice.

"We will be departing for New Province with the Helgatites. Request permission to repower the beam."

"Permission granted."

"Lone Sentinel clear."

But instead of Trust Control signing off as Erik expected, the voice came back, "Erik?"

Never had Erik heard Trust Control refer even to his father by his first name.

"Yes?" he answered just as unofficially.

"We have a complex situation here. Wayne Burdick, a hunter who passed through the Lone Sentinel over a month ago, informed Trust Control that the Lone Sentinel was manned by only one person: the son of the careman. The Helgatites have also relayed the same information. Is this correct?"

Burdick. Burdick had told. Instead of feeling angry or betrayed, Erik felt only relief.

"That is correct, Trust Control. My father died when he fell from the sentinel last winter. I've been alone here since then."

"That is the information we received. Wayne Burdick's nieces disappeared from their foster home last week. We've been searching for them in New Province, but two days ago he discovered that his notes and the maps of your area were missing. He suspected his nieces had tried to reach the Lone Sentinel. Yesterday he left New Province on an unauthorized search."

"The girls were here," Erik said. "They're with the Helgatites." How could he explain all that had taken place?

"There will be much to discuss when you arrive in New Province, Erik. An investigation team has been dispatched to the Lone Sentinel. They estimate their arrival tomorrow morning. They will assess the situation there."

"I understand."

"Trust Control clear."

"Lone Sentinel clear."

Erik mechanically repowered the beam, precisely performing each procedure without thinking. He left Maag's remains where they lay. Thursday growled at the silver suit and refused to enter the shed. The sickening odor still hovered inside the building. The investigators could decide what to do with the last of Maag.

Back inside his house, Erik removed the photograph of himself and his parents from the wall and placed it in his pack. He put in two changes of clothes and a book about Azure's wildlife that his mother had given him for his ninth birthday.

That done, he walked through the familiar house where he'd spent his entire life, and stood in the center of each room, remembering everything he could that had happened there: his mother, his father, all of them together.

With a piece of rope, he made another, stronger, leash for Thursday. He wouldn't leave without her, not this time. As he braided the rope, he thought of the videos he'd seen of Earth's long-ago ghost towns, with their eerie winds and desolately banging doors. Had too much of the biosote been destroyed for the Trust to maintain the Lone Sentinel?

Erik closed and locked the door of the house. He snapped the stout new leash to Thursday's collar and led her to the edge of the landing site. The beam whirred above them, raised to eighty-four degrees for the Helgatite landing. There wasn't even a depression in the earth where Pod 56-H had rested. The landing site was clear, ready for the true Helgatites to land.

Thursday shook her head in irritation and pawed at her ears. Erik looked up to see the descending major ship of the Helgatites. It dropped from the sky at an angle, its nose pointed into the air. It was large, very large. When the ship was at the height of the beam, it straightened and descended belly first.

Erik backed farther from the perimeter of the landing site, holding tight to Thursday's rope. He wouldn't risk her attacking the real Helgatites.

As the major ship hovered above the Lone Sentinel

compound, Erik was afraid it might be too big for the site; but finally it gently settled within the marked area. Thursday nervously pulled on the end of her rope, trying to circle Erik's legs.

"Sit, Thursday," he said. "They won't hurt us, not these aliens."

Landing arms dropped from the undercarriage and stabilized the ship, adjusting for the slightly uneven earth. The engines shut down.

The Helgatite major ship was a larger version of the transport that had landed on the plain. A door in the side of the ship opened. Shadows moved inside the ship as the ramp slid to the ground.

Thursday's tail wagged furiously, hitting against Erik's leg. She barked twice and tugged forward.

Holding hands and smiling widely, Willa and Augusta descended the ramp. Thursday strained on her leash, her rear swaying under the gyrations of her wagging tail.

"Erik!" Augusta called.

"Thursday!" shouted Willa.

Erik ran forward to meet them. Augusta's injuries were gone. Her short dark hair was combed back from her face, and the deep gash in her head had disappeared. Augusta threw her arms around Erik, laughing.

"You're all right," Erik said, holding her by the shoulders and searching her face.

"And *you're* all right," Augusta said. "They said you were, but I couldn't really believe it until I saw you myself."

"Everyone's all right," Willa said, kneeling beside Thursday. Thursday squirmed in her arms like a puppy.

Willa smiled at Erik. "I'm happy to see you, Erik," she said.

Erik stared at her. She was different. Her gaze met his fully, not wandering on past him into a world only she saw. And though her face was still gentle, it was more animated, more like Augusta's.

"You've changed," Erik told her.

Willa nodded. "The Helgatites. There was a pressure inside my head from when I fell as a little girl. They released it."

"Erik, I agree with Willa and Augusta. I couldn't be happier that you're safe."

Erik hadn't seen Burdick descend the ramp, but now he eagerly shook Burdick's offered hand. Aside from looking tired, Burdick was the same as when Erik had last seen him. The bright blue eyes and sandy hair, his tanned and wrinkled face, the broad smile.

"The Trust said you were on your way. How did you get into the Helgatite ship?"

"We picked Uncle Wayne up along the road," Willa said. "This time, *he* had to leave his vehicle behind."

Burdick laughed. "It was quite a ride on that ship. Never done anything like it. We've also got one of the investigators with us to man the sentinel until the others get here tomorrow."

Erik looked around him. "Where is he?"

Burdick held a hand to his mouth and spoke from behind it. "Doing paperwork inside. Too many rules and forms as far as I'm concerned. I have a feeling that after this incident is investigated, there will be some major changes in the Trust Control procedures."

"We're going to live with Uncle Wayne," Augusta

said. She couldn't seem to stop smiling.

"I'd be pleased if you'd stay with us until everything is sorted out, Erik," Burdick said. "You and Thursday."

"Are you sure?" Erik asked. "I've never been to New Province. I don't know anything about it—how to live, I mean."

"We'll show you," Augusta said. "You'll catch on fast enough."

The two Helgatites who'd been in the transport stood at the bottom of the ramp. Three more stood inside the door. Erik bowed to them.

"Careman Erik, you acted bravely."

"Are the Duveans destroyed?"

"Yes," said the taller Helgatite. "We gave them an opportunity to surrender, but they chose to do battle."

"And the battle on your planet?"

"The Duveans have retreated."

Erik looked up toward the blackened biosote fields. "The other sentinels . . . was their biosote destroyed too?"

"No. We were fortunate. Maag was overconfident enough to think he could destroy all the biosote on Azure with one pod and eight Duveans."

"I'd say he underestimated the bravery of our caremen," Burdick said.

"Maag always felt the colonists of Azure were inferior. It was part of the original difficulties with him," the Helgatite explained.

"We're not exactly at the top of the heap in technology." Burdick pointed to the major ship. "Just think what a difference it would make if we had airships again, especially to deliver supplies . . . "

"And carry hunting parties," Augusta added.

"Right," Burdick agreed, grinning. "You could get from New Province to here in a few minutes. No one would have to be remote."

"All of this will be taken into consideration," the Helgatite said. He turned to Erik. "Aside from your poor judgment after your father's death, Careman Erik, you have tended the Lone Sentinel well."

The Helgatite beckoned them toward the ship's ramp. "Come. We must go to New Province now. We are not prepared to spend an overly long time in your atmosphere."

The Helgatites stood beside the ramp. Burdick entered first. Thursday walked willingly beside Willa.

Erik held Augusta's hand until she entered the ship ahead of him. At the top of the ramp, he turned to look back at his home, at his empty house, at the beam above the slender tower, at Green Grass Ridge and the hills beyond the compound. He inhaled deeply of the fragrant spring growth.

The taller Helgatite stood by the door. His gloved hand hovered above Erik but didn't touch him.

"Don't worry, Careman Erik," the Helgatite said. "This will all be here when you return."

Erik looked questioningly at the Helgatite, afraid he'd heard him wrong.

"When I return?" he asked.

"When you return," the Helgatite repeated, "if you decide that's what you want."

Erik glanced once more at the rotating beam and stepped through the door into the Helgatite ship.